MURDERER'S WAKE

A Novel

By J.C. Alonso, Jr.

NORTHAMPTON HOUSE PRESS

First edition 2018 by Northampton House Press. Cover by Naia Poyer.
ISBN 978-1-937997-84-7
Library of Congress Control Number: 2017946892

10 9 8 7 6 5 4 3

Who shall cross the sea
but he whose heart is set
on a course he cannot escape?

— *Bernardim Ribeiro*

PROLOGUE

The impact, after falling from the deck, and the cool, salty water opened his eyes. The back of his head hurt. A weight was dragging him down. He was tangled . . . and sinking . . . and needed air. Someone had hit him, he remembered.

When he struggled to the surface muffled voices were arguing somewhere above, fading in the night. Chains and shackles clattered. An engine rumbled, a propeller rotated steadily beneath the surface, and the pulsations pulled at his bowels.

He tried to shout a curse, but the sea filled his mouth and his throat and air bubbles went up where he wanted to go. And so, all that came out with the bubbles was a croaked "– you." He shouted it again, in Spanish, adding a direr threat, but his voice was weaker now. He looked up at the ship. It was smaller against the stars. Darker. A speck. Were they looking back at him? He was sinking. Or was it just receding, leaving him? Proceeding on its appointed course, oblivious to the enormous wrong that was happening?

The pain hit then, goring his side, and he put his hand to his rib, to feel the piercing. Warmth mingled with the cold of the sea. No wonder he was weakening. He stopped swimming. Called, in a hoarse croak, "Papi. Papi – "

When he surfaced again the ship was gone.

The deep sea felt colder now. It was making him sleepy. He gestured feebly with his hands, sculling. He forgot where he was, then came to again. Was that the ship or a big fish?

He struggled, quivered, holding his breath. Veins bulging, his mouth gulping like a dying goldfish. Holding on to life. Alone, on the calm Caribbean. Another desperate moment, gulping.

Then the blackness of the depths sucked him in.

1:
DEAD RECKONING

My name is Cesar Santino. This is my story . . . why I left home for the ship and the sea, and then, left the sea as well. I tell it to set the record straight, despite reports that may surface.

My father had charted my course for me. "Forget the navy. Forget the merchant marine. Go to college—be a lawyer—a doctor—a professional," he'd bark. Dad was an old salt. He'd retired from the navy to become a cargo ship captain. He cherished the sea, yet feared its wrath. He wanted a different life for his sons.

And so, I set aside the Blue Book and dreams of becoming an officer, and graduated from college with a bachelor's degree in English. I was accepted to graduate school (in philosophy, but I told the old man it was law school). But my younger half-brother, Roby, was determined to be a merchant sailor. After he finished high school, he went to sea with Dad.

I got the call on an August morning. I was jogging through campus, with the last of the pink azaleas and white dogwood blossoms littering the sidewalks and trails. Students buzzed among them like bees. The fraternity and sorority houses were busy chasing and recruiting. New faces flirted and giggled as I ran by in sweat pants and a tank top. It was my second year on the boxing team. I'd spend a few hours in the gym on the heavy bag or the speed bag, then off to the library to read Kant, Hegel, and Nietzsche. A steady rhythm, mind and body floating along as one. My life's course appeared set.

And not much different from all the eager faces around me. They bragged about the bridges they'd build, the actors or models they'd become, the concerts and symphonies they'd perform, and all the money they were going to make. The campus sizzled with impetuous wanna-bes.

My favorite street to jog on was University Park. On one side, Bob's book store clamored with lines of students talking about what classes to take, who the best teachers were, or who banged who the night before. On the other side, sorority row.

During the last two weeks of August, the sisters gathered in front of the two-story houses, on the manicured lawns, to recruit pledges. In front of the Tri-Delta House, a little blonde stepped out to halt me as I jogged by. She had emerald green eyes—like the island-waters of the Caribbean. A petite thing; the top of her head reached the middle of my chest. She smiled, revealed dimples, as I jogged in place. "Hey... doing anything tonight? There's a party here; it starts at eight—it's—Friday—you—know."

"Yeah, I know it's Friday."

"Does that mean you're coming?"

"Yeah . . . I'll come."

"Good, I'll look for you around eight, or nine." Then a smug nod, and without saying her name—or asking mine—she turned back to the other girls.

What a clever little mystery. I kept jogging toward the gym with Ms. no-name island-eyes etched in my thoughts. Squirrels scrambled from my path and up the oaks toward the invasion of chirping robins that accompanied the new faces each fall. I powered up the grade to the university entrance. Inside the circular drive, a white marble fountain sprayed water. Twice around to cool off in the splatter, then up the wide sidewalk to the building that housed the English Department and Philosophy Department. Then I'd follow the sidewalk down the gentle slope to the gym.

I sprinted up the front steps and to the weight room at the end of the corridor. Next to it was a gym for the boxing team with a regulation ring in the center and bags in the corners. I busted through the front doors. My coach held the heavy bag for an enraged animal who made me glad to be in the middleweight class. "Let's go, kid; you're ten minutes late again," he shouted at me.

"Yes sir."

"Chasing skirts—again? Third time this week, kid! Young. Dumb. Full of cum!"

"Yes sir." He was stuck on that line. He said it two or three times a day. He was in his fifties, ex-Marine, shaved head, grayish goatee.

"No time to tape up—just use the braces. Move it, kid! Think I got all day for you?"

"Yes . . . I mean, no sir."

"You're done, go cool off," he told the animal. To me, "Come on now. Step in here. Hit the friggin' bag! Snap the left in. Snap it in there. That's right! Stick it in there . . . Keep your right up when you jab. Don't drop it when you strike. You leave yourself open."

"Yes sir."

"Drop that right hand one more time, I'm gonna tape it to your head. You understand?"

He barked at me for half an hour, then sounded off on the next guy. I caught my breath, chugged an energy drink, and pounded out a couple of hours on the speed bag. A thirty minute break. Chugged a protein-shake for lunch, then hit the weight room until my calves and thighs burned. Late that afternoon, a slow, sweat-drenched trot home. Forget the library—go to the party—the blonde—those green eyes.

When I reached my dorm, the sun had smeared an orange haze against the cloudy dark horizon. But there was a note on my door. It read *answer your phone*. No signature.

When I put my cell to my ear, a woman was sobbing on the other end. "Mom? Mom—what's wrong?"

"Cesar—finally. Your father's been trying to reach you since breakfast. Your brother's missing."

"Missing? What do you mean he's missing, Mom?"

"As far as anyone can tell, he fell overboard last night." She started crying. Listening to her cry made my eyes start to swell up. I waited for her to gather herself. "I don't really know much more. Just wait for your father to call. He's still aboard. He'll try you again around nine." She started crying again and muttered that she loved me and that she was going to hang up.

"OK, Mom—love you, too." How could this be? Could Roby be hiding? Clinging to a buoy? He couldn't be dead. How could this have happened? I threw off my shirt, kicked off my shoes and sweat pants, and lay down on the bed in my jock strap. I stared at the ceiling. Tears filled my eyes. My little brother . . . overboard?

Roberto Santino had turned seventeen that June. A great athlete, he'd been nominated All City in baseball as a catcher.

He'd also been on the swimming team his freshman year in high school. He couldn't have drowned. Well, who knows—waves— sharks. I wished Dad would call. What time was it? I wiped my eyes. Twenty minutes to go. My head filled with images of Roby drowning. How could this be? I tried to forget the vision of my brother sinking in the ocean. But everywhere I saw his face. The ceiling, the walls, the door all became the deep blue ocean with all its predators, swallowing my brother, helplessly snarled and yelping in the sea.

Then a knock at the door; I didn't move. Couldn't answer. It came louder and longer—determined and stronger. As in Poe's "Raven", death was knocking. Get up and face it.

"Cesar? Your father's on the phone downstairs," a soft voice said.

The dorm phone? Why wasn't be calling my cell? "OK, I'm coming." Her footsteps faded down the hall. I threw on the same sweaty shirt and sweatpants, and padded barefoot down to the old front desk. The receiver lay on a stack of fall curriculums. I took a deep breath. "Yeah, Dad, I'm here."

"Cesar, good to get hold of you. I know you spoke to your mother. Just got off the phone with her again."

"Well, tell me."

"Your brother's still missing. His body hasn't been recovered."

"What happened?"

"Don't know, Cesar. I'm having a . . . rough time with it. We arrived at the mouth of Port Everglades around 0100. Received a dispatch that the pier was jammed, and to wait outside the channel. We let go in the shipping lanes and waited for the pilot. He showed around 0500 and took her in. Not until we docked did I realize he was missing."

7

"Nobody heard or saw anything?"

"The cook said Roby came by the galley around 0200, picked up a bucket of squid and went aft. Gordo left him sitting on a pin at the bitts fishing with a hand spool. Everyone else was below decks, or asleep . . . except for the chief mate and a helmsman on the bridge."

"This is hard to believe, Dad."

"Well, I was between my cabin and the comm room. The helmsman stayed on the bridge with the chief. We wouldn't have heard anything from the stern."

"This is unbelievable."

"The Coast Guard's continuing the search from the fix we anchored at, north towards Ft. Lauderdale—the current would've pulled him up the coast. We're praying someone picked him up or he swam in somewhere, but it doesn't look good. It's been almost twenty-four hours now."

"His body hasn't turned up—right? So there's still a chance."

"Sure—always a chance—but. . . . "

"This doesn't make sense! Someone has to know something!"

"Listen, Son, I've been over this with the Port Authority, the police, the Coast Guard and your mother all day today. Don't need this from you."

"Yes sir. How long will you be ashore?"

"Well, your mother's blaming me. So, I'll stay a month. A relief captain will take over. The best thing for you is to come home and be with your mother."

"I could leave in the morning."

"The Coast Guard's doing all it can. Come home."

"OK, Dad." He hung up and I did too. Blew out, and looked blankly at the stack of free stuff people left by the door. Fans. Old sweat shirts. Old shoes.

Discarded stuff. Thrown away.

I went to my room and showered, then powered up my notebook and emailed the chair of the Philosophy Department and my boxing coach, the Marine.

The next morning, I threw my luggage in my rusted truck and left. But not for home. It was the right choice—the only choice.

Something didn't add up, and the answer was aboard that ship.

2:
PROMISE

Morning came with an overcast sky; the air smelled of dew. I sputtered south in my old truck. It rained the whole drive. Sometimes drizzle, other times blinding downpours.

I pulled into Mom's driveway a few hours after dark, parked next to the basketball post, and listened to the wipers squeak. Roby and I had dug the hole and cemented in the 6 x 4 when he was still in grade school. We didn't wear gloves, and we both got splinters. The rim was only nine feet tall and bent from all the dunking I'd practiced. Later, in high school, he'd started dunking, too. I remembered the gleam in his eyes. He'd grown up fast.

I thought back to the day I'd broken his lip with an elbow. He tackled me. We wrestled until I pinned him. When I let go, he was so mad, he tried to box with me. He was stronger every year after that.

Too strong to fall overboard and drown.

When I slammed the truck door, Skipper sounded off. The English bulldog's oversized head appeared between the curtains. His low-pitched bark seemed weaker. On the front porch, a dozen moths circled the bright yellow lamp. Another dozen lay dead beneath it on the terrazzo. Fern baskets hung wilted. The front door opened. I scarcely recognized the woman who opened it: hair much grayer, skin gaunt, lacking the glow of Florida's sunshine. The puffy black circles under her eyelids contrasted with pale cheeks. She fumbled with the keys to the iron security gate. The bulldog recognized me and wagged his docked tail like a severed digit. The dog bumped into her as she inserted the key. It jammed. I reached through the bars and took the key ring. "Let me do it, Mom."

She sighed. "It's good to have you home again." Skipper slipped past before I could shut the iron gate. He went straight to my truck, circled it, then pissed on my back tire—nice greeting. I hugged her until she let go.

The muscle-bound bulldog marched back in. I locked the gate and the door. "Has Dad been by yet?"

"No. He said maybe tomorrow."

"Well, I'm going over there early, to see what I can find out."

She pretended not to hear. "You must be hungry. I made some sandwiches." She turned toward the kitchen. I followed. The dog jumped up to greet me. I slapped his big head and mashed his wet nostrils. He snarled and growled, then slobbered his pink tongue over my hands.

The dining room was dark except for a candle. It glowed next to a photo of Roby propped on the desk next to the telephone. Throughout my childhood, she'd lit many candles for my father when a hurricane crossed the Gulf, or he hadn't called when he promised to—ship overdue. A flickering candle in a dark room makes me think about the person who lit it . . . the fragile hope inherent in the gesture . . . the ease with which a flame, or a life, can go out.

She brought a plate with tuna sandwiches neatly cut in halves and stacked, and sat across from me. Her eyes darted to the photograph, then to me. I reached for a sandwich and took a bite.

"It's been over forty-eight hours now. He's gone." A sudden tear trickled down one cheek and she quickly wiped both eyes with a crumpled napkin in her palm. "The ocean's taken him." Her voice quivered. "The sea has always been against me. Your father spent most of our marriage out there. And now, it's stolen one of my sons."

Our eyes met again. I took another bite and passed her the plate. She took a small bite and left the rest, then sighed, wiped her face again, and wedged her palms on the table to help her stand. "Don't answer the phone if it rings—just let the machine pick up. There was something on the news about it, so his high school friends have been calling."

She paused. I kept eating. A snout nudged my leg. I tossed Skipper a corner of the sandwich. He gobbled it and licked my hand. "I'm glad you're home, but I'm going to try and sleep now." She wobbled over to me and kissed my forehead. Then she walked off toward her room; her slippers shuffling.

I thought of a line from the poem Reluctance: ...*when was it ever less than treason, to accept the end and bow to reason.* She paused at her door and looked back at me.

"I'm leaving for the port first thing in the morning," I said. "I'll find out what happened to him. I promise, Mom."

"I heard you the first time, Cesar." She closed the door.

3:
M/V *CARIBBEAN TRADER*

I left before she woke. I didn't want to explain my plans, nor was I completely sure yet what they were. Perhaps Dad could drive my truck back to stay with her, so I could board. I remembered he'd said he might stay. I hoped he would sail. It would make things easier, but either way, I wanted answers.

There wasn't much traffic Sunday mornings on the Palmetto Expressway. Weekdays it jammed for miles between the hours of seven and nine. The sky was gray. It looked like rain again.

Port Everglades was just south of Fort Lauderdale in Dania and over an hour from home. I followed I-95 North, and turned on State Road 84 heading toward the ocean. Four red and white smokestacks marked the port. The entrance channel was on the north end and the larger cargo terminals were there, or at the south point where the roll-on/roll-off ships could maneuver. The Midport docks had enormous berth areas for the cruise ship lines. The facility resembled an airline terminal with canvas causeways extended to each ship. On one of my previous trips,

Queen Elizabeth II had been on her way out through the Intracoastal when our ship was coming in. It'd felt like we were in a canoe when we glided by her in the channel.

At the administration building, I found out which terminal Dad's ship was moored at. The Northport terminals, 6 through 16, were all cargo and included a mile or two of slips. I had no way of knowing which one. After identifying myself and acquiring a pass to Terminal #7, I drove to the pier, and showed the security at the guard house my pass.

"What's the ship's name, Bubba?"

"Caribbean Trader—I'm Captain Santino's son."

"What?" A twinkle of hope crossed his face.

"His oldest son."

"Oh…. go ahead. There's another guard posted in front of the gangplank—they've tightened up. So bring your ID. I hope they find your brother." He tipped his cap and I drove in.

The entire port must've been on alert over the incident. I drove along the fence-line and made a left in front of the warehouses. A super-sized fork lift pulled out in front of me carrying a twenty-foot red and blue container. I followed cautiously, keeping ten truck lengths between us. I felt like a roach scurrying along trying not to be squashed. The mammoth CAT stopped at an orange ship named *Nordic Prince,* and I swerved quickly around.

Next was *Caribbean Trader.* The ship was painted in two tones: dark navy blue from the gunwales down to the 30 foot draft mark and rustic red to the waterline and underneath. I stopped next to the cleat the bowline was tied to. The ram-bow sat high on the water—she was empty. As soon as I parked, the security guard started walking toward me.

14

I showed my pass and ID. "Cesar Santino. Captain Santino's oldest son."

He checked my pass, read my ID, and looked in my eyes. "Go on up—you have my condolences." He was in his sixties, but fit. His uniform and the pistol strapped to his side gave him an imposing presence. "Watch yourself on the way up."

The gangplank had at least a fifty-five degree pitch. The tide up and the ship empty made the climb my first chore. Gangplanks have small metal wheels dockside, so they can adjust with the flow and ebb of the tide. The walking surface has 1x2 raised wooden strips every twelve inches for traction. I gripped the coarse hemp lines threaded through iron rods, pushed my toes down on the strips, and pulled up the forty foot platform, over the gunwale, down the small step ladder, and onto the steel deck.

A sailor stood watch. "Quien buscas?" he said.

"Captain Santino."

"El Capitán….Esta en su cabina." He'd told me what I already figured—Dad was in his cabin. I knew the way.

I glanced down, along the open hatch covers toward the bow. The ship was exactly 532 feet length over all. The captain had drilled this into my skull. *Caribbean Trader* was a bulkcarrier. It had a single deck with six cargo holds and six hydraulic hatch covers. A double-set of mast poles with a derrick winch stationed in between every two holds. Each post had two booms—two for the starboard side and two for the port side. And each boom had a radius of about fifty feet. The stack and castle were aft with huge windows on the bridge to oversee everything. She was old, but a great ship; I knew every square foot of her.

15

The castle, living quarters, had five levels above the main deck. The old man's cabin was on the fourth. I walked up the cramped ladderway and knocked on his open door.

"Go ahead," his familiar voice called. His cabin had two sections. On the right side, bunk and head, and on the left a large rectangular table that seated eight—he sat at the top. Nautical charts piled the far end. He was at his desk, staring into the screen of the bolted-down computer. Above him on the bulkhead was a photograph of a lighthouse in Spain near the village where he was born. Breakfast hadn't been cleared away, yet a bottle of Chivas Regal stood on the table and an empty glass beside it.

He pushed back from the keyboard when he saw me. "Well, Son, you made it."

"Yes sir, Dad. How are you?"

"Come in. Sit down. Want me to ring the cook to fix you some eggs?"

"No, I'll grab one of those bananas and some coffee. That's enough."

"How's your mom?" His eyes were bloodshot beneath salt and pepper hair. He stroked a black mustache.

"Upset."

"The Coast Guard was here at seven. They've searched the coastline and turned up nothing. They've filed Roby as a missing person."

"Nothing? Not even his shirt?"

"Lots of sharks in these waters, Son. They're gonna keep looking. Something'll eventually turn up."

"I find it hard to believe he just fell over and vanished."

"So do I. But the police interrogated the entire crew. The only person who saw him was the cook when he got bait to go

16

fish. Everyone was asleep by three except for the chief and the helmsman, on the bridge. I was probably in here. I've already told you this."

"I need a break from school. I wanna crew-up this trip."

"How is school?"

"Good."

"Still boxing?"

"Yes, sir."

"If you need some time off—I understand. But I need to be with your mother. And, I need a break from the sea. Captain McMorris is taking over. You remember him?"

"Yeah. I know him."

"Well, it's up to him. I'm staying ashore for a month—or until the ship returns. He'll be aboard soon."

He reached for the bottle, glanced at me, and unscrewed the cap. He raised his eyebrows. I didn't say anything. I could smell the scotch across the table—strong but sweet. His thin, ruddy face held no expression. He filled a third of the glass, meticulously turned the cap back on, and then licked his forefinger and thumb. He wore his white uniform shirt with four gold bands on the shoulder loops. When he wore it, people treated him differently. It was unbuttoned, creased. Gray hair protruded from the v-shaped sunburn his t-shirt left. His fine grizzling hair was parted on his left side and in need of trimming—it fell over his wrinkled forehead. He brushed it back, rubbed the stubble on his cheeks, gulped half the glass he'd poured, and smacked his lips. "So, how is law school?"

The question I'd dreaded. I glanced at the Chivas and cleared my throat. "Dad, I . . . postponed that. For now. I was accepted into grad school, though—in philosophy."

"Philosophy? You'll starve."

17

"I can teach."

"Hell, all those abstract conjectures about stuff we have no control over. Doing—that's the only philosophy I know. For me, it's always been the sea."

"Mom holds it against you, I think."

"That's why we separated. We both still care though. Well, a man's got to steer his own course. You are enrolled in something, though—right?"

"Yes, sir. I'll just take this semester off , and go back in January."

"All right, I won't argue. Do as you like. I'll put a word in for you with McMorris." He slurped down the rest of the scotch and leaned back in his chair with his ritual palm-smack of the table. "It'll be a good trip across the puddle." He always called the Gulf of Mexico a puddle. The Atlantic and the Pacific, those were oceans. "I spoke to Fernandez at the office. The ship is going to Houston again, then back to La Guaira. After that, a couple weeks in Curaçao's dry-dock. The rudder has been slipping, the winch on number two hold needs a new drive, and three ballast tanks on the port side are rotted through. And hell, might as well paint the hull. And you know what? As of yesterday, I'm two seamen short: a deckhand and an oiler. Spooked, I guess."

Working the deck might be a good place to start my search. "You could take my truck to mom's. But I still have my bag in it."

"Sure are determined to go. But I don't know what you think you can accomplish."

A knock at the door. "Captain." A tall, heavy-set, sunburnt Anglo walked in. He stepped to the table and shook Dad's hand.

18

"Sorry about the circumstances, Captain Santino. I was informed at the home office."

"Yes, thank you—it has been difficult. You know my oldest?"

"Of course. He was a pup last time I saw him." McMorris was in his late sixties and fat. He was balding but grew out what hair he did have on the sides and back. A pair of gold-rimmed Ray-Bans was propped over a pink forehead and he smelled like coconut lotion. A colorful short-sleeved Hawaiian shirt draped broad shoulders and a beer belly. Khaki shorts covered his oversized buttocks and leather boat moccasins were swelled out from his weight. The left pocket of his shirt was stuffed with papers, pens, and an eyeglass case. He set his briefcase in a chair, reached across, and clutched my hand in his paw. Then grunted and dropped his weight into the chair beside the briefcase.

A tap at the door, and the steward appeared with a sailor standing beside him. Each carried a large suitcase. They set the luggage down just inside the entranceway, and glanced at Pop. He nodded. McMorris didn't turn to look, but watched my dad. They wanted to talk alone, so I excused myself and left the cabin.

The rest of the morning I reacquainted myself with the ship; back and forth through the narrow passageways and up to the bridge. The ladderway ended where the chartroom started. On the chart desk, the Gulf of Mexico was sprawled out and weighed down with a protractor and slide-ruler. The ship had all the digital stuff, but Dad still liked paper. The desktop was made of glass and eight feet long. The dark teak drawers were shallow with brass handles and almost as long as the desk. I opened the door to the bridge and hooked it to the bulkhead. My steps echoed in the enclosed empty wheelhouse. Teak wood with

19

brass rivets framed each window. Old, but solid. I strolled out on the port wing.

The Intracoastal was busy. A steady gust was blowing in off the ocean and the sky remained overcast. But two thirty-foot fishing boats were moving out. Aboard a Mako with twin Yamaha outboards two girls in bikinis drank beer and swayed to reggae music. It was followed by a Wellcraft with twin 150 Mercs. Two woman were lying on its bow sunbathing. Both boats had outriggers up and one guy in each boat was rigging bait. They all waved at me as they went by. I watched the white foam from their wake. Seagulls followed them out through the channel on the salty wind.

It would be easier to stay; to simply accept things as they happened. As Dad said—what did I hope to accomplish? I wondered how Mom was getting along today. She needed answers; I needed them, too. The ship held them. How could he just have fallen? He wasn't stupid or clumsy. I was obsessed. Someone knew something. Someone had to. I'd work the deck and anything else I could do. Talk to everyone until they were sick of my questions. Someone knew. My gaze followed the fishing boats.

A forty-foot Sea Hawk race boat passed them coming in. It rumbled past *Trader*. Three tanned, muscle-head Latino men wearing gold chains and NY baseball caps stood behind the wheel. They weren't drinking. They had no fishing poles and didn't bother to wave at me. I watched the bright yellow boat before as it disappeared down the waterway. On the starboard side, in large black letters, was the boat's name, *MY VICE*.

I watched boats for several hours: a fifty-foot schooner, a Hobie-Cat, and a Boston Whaler with a pole in every rod holder.

Trailing behind the Whaler, two little dinghies raced side-by-side; the harbor patrol blasted the horn at them in the channel.

One of Crowley's large container ships came through the mouth of the Intracoastal. It passed alongside *Trader* heading toward South Point to maneuver. It was a RO/RO vessel; the bridge and castle were toward the bow. It took an experienced harbor pilot to reverse the ship in the turning notch. I waited until she reached the point. Then, I raced inside the bridge, grabbed the binoculars, hurried back to my spot, and rested my elbows on the railing for steady focus.

The pilot's launch blew its horn three times and left a blue strobe light revolving to stop traffic. The vessel let go the portside anchor and out thundered the giant chain against the thru-hull echoing up and down the waterway. Water splashed up twenty feet. Sailors scrabbled on the fo'c'sle. Gradually, it turned with the wind and the current. When it lined up with the pier, water blasted out from beneath the bow and then bubbled forth as the thrusters engaged. Slowly, the stern moved in reverse.

On cue, two tandem tugboats appeared from around the South point. The red and green team (tied together as one) touched the ship's stern on the starboard side. Black diesel fumes filled the air as they adjusted the heavy ship's leeward drift. The ship remained motionless in counterbalance between the thrusters and the tugboats while the windlass heaved the anchor aboard. Finally, anchor secured, the stern gate began opening to meet the concrete platform. The tugboats nudged the ship until the mooring lines were made fast, then the team disappeared around the point again. The procedure lasted less than an hour. I returned the binoculars to the case, unlatched the door between the bridge and the chart room, closed it, and made my way down the ladderway to the captain's cabin.

The steward came out with a suitcase. Dad followed, a windbreaker over his shoulder, briefcase in hand. "Ok, Son, Captain McMorris agreed. You are signed on as an ordinary seaman—a deckhand. Give him your passport and he'll inform the home office before the ship leaves tonight."

"Thanks, Dad. I'll walk down with you. My truck's near the bow."

At my pickup, I retrieved my bag and tossed him the keys. "Tell Mom I'll send her a postcard from Venezuela. Oh, and I left my computer behind the seat. Put it in my room for me, okay? I've got all my class stuff on it."

He nodded, searching his pocket, then extended his arm as if to shake hands. Instead, he shoved a watch into my palm. "This was for your brother. I think you should keep it."

I turned it over in my fingers. It was a waterproof Seiko diver's watch with a bright blue face plate, tachometer, and a depth range of 500 ft. I took off my beat up Timex, handed it to him, and said to leave it in the glove box. We shook hands. Then with his left he shuffled my long, dirty-blond hair and quickly slapped the side of my face with a right hook. "Do not drop your guard out there," he said. Then turned, opened the noisy, rusted door to my old truck, cranked it, and sputtered past the warehouses.

I stood on the pier until he reached the far gate. My stomach fluttered. In the past, he'd always been there—the captain. It'd always been the beginning of summer, not the fall. As he disappeared, I turned and dragged my duffel up the gangway.

I was a sailor again.

4:
THE GALLEY

I went back to the skipper's cabin to turn in my passport. The door stood open and the steward was inside delivering linen. "Excuse me, Captain McMorris."

"Come in, Cesar. Shipping out with us, huh?" His suitcase lay opened on top of the bunk. He was stowing clothes in the drawers of the cabinet, his back to me.

"Yes, sir, thank you. Here's my passport. I lost my old seaman's card."

He pointed to the table. "No worries. Your father tells me you've been going to sea with him since the age of seven." He continued walking between the bunk and the cabinet. He had thick, round, calf muscles like a football player and the back of his fair-skinned legs were burnt pink like his face. "He says you know your way around a ship. And that you're a half decent helmsman, too."

"The Virgin Islands was my first trip, sir. I was seasick that trip—first and last time. Earned my seaman's card at 22. Worked the deck of bulk carriers, especially this one."

"Good to have you with us. I'm still short an oiler, plus the chief engineer has never had a third officer. Your father informed me that one of the helmsmen could sub as the third oiler. That may give you a shift at the wheel."

"Whatever you need, sir."

"Well, go see the chief mate and he'll get you situated. Do you know him?"

"It's been two years since I've been on this ship. What's his name?"

"He's called El Soldado. He's from Peru, quite a character; a military man."

"No sir. I don't think I've met him."

McMorris finished stuffing drawers, pulled a bottle of Old Spice, a toothbrush, and an electric shaver from the suitcase, and heaved himself into the head. His voice echoed in the small space. "The chief sailed with me as my second mate a few years back. Then your father needed a first officer. He tested and passed….I guess it was three years ago. Yeah, that sounds about right. Anyways, go see him."

"Yes sir. Thanks again, Captain McMorris." I lifted my luggage, flexed my triceps, and stepped into the passageway.

I wondered how many crew members I did know. I'd said it'd been two years, but it was probably closer to four because of college, and I'd always sailed in summertime.

Roby's watch read eleven o'clock. This meant the cook had to be getting lunch ready. It was always served at eleven-thirty. That never changed. And most important, the cook had been the last to see Roby alive.

First, I walked past the ladderway. The captain's quarters were on the starboard side of the fourth level. On the port side, beginning from the ladderway, the first, the second, and the third mate's cabins were lined in descending order. Above, on the fifth level, behind the bridge and alone on the port side, was the radioman's cabin.

The chief mate's door was closed. Usually sailors closed a door when they didn't want to be disturbed. Otherwise, a twelve-inch straight steel hook would be latched. It hung from the bulkhead and slipped into an eye ring screwed into the door frame. This cracked the door slightly to provide an air stream between the cabin's porthole and the passageway. If it was latched open, you could knock. I'd learned this long ago. I didn't knock and left my suitcase outside the captain's cabin against the bulkhead and a few feet from the doorway; no one would mess with it there. I turned down the ladderway.

The galley was three decks below the captain's quarters and as far astern as possible. The crew's mess was directly in front of it, but on the starboard side. The officer's mess was also to starboard, but one level above the crew's mess and galley.

I'd learned two other basic things years ago. First, you always want to be on the cook's good side. This could get you many fringe benefits; such as, fruit at night and after meals, second and third helpings, and first choice of leftovers. The second thing to remember was that rivalries always existed among the crew, so it was best to stay neutral as long as possible. The place to exercise both these lessons was the galley.

The captain was the supreme master of the ship, but the cook ruled the galley. The last time I'd sailed on *Caribbean Trader* the cook had been Sergio. He was Mexican, weighed almost three hundred pounds, and was affectionately called Gordo. If he was aboard, he'd be a good ally.

I hurried below deck. I hadn't forgotten about Roby, but at the same time, knowing I'd soon be on the open sea filled me with excitement. It was the only thing I felt good about. The same way I'd felt on my first voyage to the Virgin Islands—like a child on Christmas morning opening gifts…like the way I felt about the little blond with the green eyes, or the very first instant you realize the one you want, wants you. I wanted to look out at nothing but the blue sea. I felt summoned.

From below rose the sweet aroma of plantains frying in grease. Gordo always cooked plantains for lunch. This was a good sign. Sure enough, in front of the smoking-hot stoves a familiar obese figure stirred a giant frying pan. Hearing my footsteps, he turned.

"Mira quien es—cabron." Gordo didn't speak a word of English. And, no matter what the circumstances might be, he always smiled. He'd been born and raised in Juarez, Mexico. Early death was nothing strange to him. His parents had died when he was still young; gang violence had taken his brothers; his only sister had died of a heroin overdose, and so he'd shipped out to sea as a cook, sworn never to return. He used to say, 'Felicidad no existe; solamente momentos feliz—There is no such thing as happiness; only happy moments.' Yet he still found reasons to smile. It was his revenge against adversity—against sorrow.

He clattered down the frying pan on a cold burner, wiped his sweaty hands on his greasy, once-white apron, plopped a stout arm around my shoulders, and hauled me in. The weight of his arm and the collision with his belly buckled my knees. He was filthy. "Good to see you Gordo." I told him in Spanish.

Then a sudden sorrow filled his pudgy face. His two gold front teeth receded under his black moustache. In a low somber tone, he immediately recounted the sequence of events that had transpired the night Roby asked him for bait to go fishing. He repeated himself several times. He swore he'd heard nothing and

26

seen nothing. He said he drank eight or nine beers that night, gave Roby five pounds of squid, and slept like the dead. (He dropped his eyes when he said dead.) He was up at five to start breakfast and found out Roby was missing after the ship docked.

I believed him. Before I let him go back to work, I asked him if the crew was the same I'd known from my last trip. He said everyone was new up on deck. The chief engineer was the same, but he had new officers. I asked him not to tell anyone who I was, just to call me Cesar. I didn't want everyone feeling sorry for me. He raised an eyebrow and wrinkled his brow. Then I told him I'd signed on as a deckhand. His gold teeth flashed again.

He turned up the heat, gripped the enormous iron pan in one plump hand, grabbed a serving spoon with the other, and stirred the plantains. I reached around the Behemoth and put my fingers into the pan before the oil boiled again. I snagged the juiciest plantain and slurped it down—greasy sweetness. He rammed his fat ass against my hip. "Cabron, ya empezaste."

The first round was mine. I had an ally.

5:
THE CREW'S MESS

I stepped back and watched Gordo work. Grease sizzled; two oversized crock pots of white rice and another huge one full of black beans simmered on the stainless-steel stove. He turned the rice so it wouldn't stick, then stirred the beans. From inside the oven, he pulled out a large, flat pan of shredded steak topped with onions, green and red peppers-- "ropa vieja" (old clothes), a favorite with Latin crews.

Sailors began stomping down the ladderway. I felt like a visitor in my clean blue jeans and tight short sleeve polo shirt.

The first three were Mexican, medium height, and looked like brothers. They had to be deckhands. Their dusty blue coveralls read Gulf Stream Shipping Company over the left pocket. Each glanced at me and sat at the far table. The steward rushed in behind them. He apparently had been above preparing the officer's mess. He was Filipino, short, slim, agile, and in his forties with straight black hair and gray-dappled side burns. His white shirt and white pants had food stains; his high-top sneakers had holes. Gordo yelled "Chino" from the galley. He spun on his heel and raced out, then returned holding a

28

steaming pot of rice by the handles, and placed it next to the three deckhands.

The biggest seized the serving spoon and piled his plate. Then the two younger ones held out theirs; he shoveled out heaping spoonfuls. Rice was the first thing everyone wanted. Even at breakfast there was always white rice; the staple of every sea crew I'd known. I waited in the passageway and let everyone else go first.

The mess room's two twenty-foot long picnic-style tables were arranged parallel to each other and draped with red and white-checked cloths. Pitchers of iced water stood near the centers. Tables and benches were bolted to the deck. Above, at the far end of the room, a TV was clamped inside a steel frame welded to the overhead. A baseball game played, but the volume had been turned down. As the catcher flashed the pitcher a sign from under his mitt, I realized Roby's watch was too tight. I loosened the snap, scratched the imprint on my skin, adjusted it, and clipped it again.

Two more sailors entered, wiping grimy hands with rags. Their coveralls, black with grease and oil, were unzipped to the navel and sweat dripped from their faces. The tall, skinny one nodded at me; the heavy-set one didn't even notice me—he went for the rice. A thin older man with a well-trimmed beard and long silvery hair in a ponytail sauntered in. He unbuckled a carpenter's belt and hung it on the coat rack. A hammer, several screwdrivers and a tape measure were strapped in the niches. Nothing fell out.

Chino toted in a tray with large bowls of black beans, one for each table. A second steward hurried down the ladderway. He was nineteen or twenty, dressed in white, with short black hair, and the same height and frame as Chino. He disappeared into the galley, returned with two platters of ropa vieja, placed one on each table, and scurried above deck. Gordo came in behind him, lodged a pot of rice and another of beans in the dumbwaiter, then pressed the button. Overhead, silverware clinked, plates clanged, footsteps and voices echoed down the ladderway. Four more sailors trotted in. They nodded, waved, or smiled as they passed. I walked in last, and sat on the end of the table closest to the entranceway.

The biggest of the three turned out to be the foreman/boatswain; someone called him Rafa, short for Rafael. Besides him, the last three were helmsmen. The one I sat next to said his name was Tomas. I introduced myself as Cesar, the new deckhand. No one asked for last names—the objective was the meal.

After that announcement, a clumsy silence infected my table. I got polite nods, strained smiles, and piercing looks. They tolerated me like a stray dog that needed a meal. The other table clamored in conversation; mine staggered in hushed talk. The food was good. I didn't mind the silence.

Then Gordo brought in the fried plantains. In a loud voice worthy of his size, he said, "Cabrones, this is Cesar, a worthless bastard of a deckhand. I sailed with him three years ago." He set the platter of plantains next to me. I scooped three on my plate and passed it down.

"Saludos, saludos." Everyone repeated the welcome and suddenly the tension melted. Rafa began talking about the relief captain. Someone said we were sailing back to Venezuela by way of Houston. Another sailor turned up the TV's volume— Yankees up two to nothing at the bottom of the second inning.

Tomas swallowed and looked at me. "So you know Gordo?"

30

"Yeah, during summers I sign on. I know Mr Fernandez at the home office on the Miami River."

He nodded and reached for the water pitcher, poured himself a full glass, filled mine, and kept eating. "Gracias," I said. He had short, curly black hair, black eyes, and buck teeth. His coveralls were splattered with bits of chipped red paint. Chips speckled his face and neck. Scuffed leather work boots were double-laced around the ankles and his pant legs were tucked inside the boots. He was in his late thirties, chubby, and about medium height.

"Rafa said we're going back to La Guaira. I'm from Maracaibo. Ever been there?"

"Yeah, but that was a while ago." I felt cornered. The more I talked, the more I revealed. "So, you work the deck?"

"At sea I'm a wheelman, but we all work the deck when we have to. The holds have ulcers." He smiled.

"Piqueta all day, right? What are we loading?" He knew I understood his little test.

"Fertilizer again—back to Houston—to grow crops to feed my country." Once again he flashed buck teeth, then slurped down a plantain and washed it down with a gulp of water.

Everyone wolfed down the food with limited conversation. Before long, a shuffle came from behind me. The three Mexican brothers got up to leave. This time one of the youngsters tapped my shoulder and disappeared; the big Mexican stared, silent. Not long after, the carpenter strapped on his belt. His leather face forced a smile and left.

My table grew silent again. Those remaining rushed their meal. I glanced at my watch; almost twelve thirty. The Yankees were still winning. Rafa and the two helmsmen stood and dragged napkins across their mouths. Rafa shook my hand and welcomed me again; the other two nodded.

Tomas jumped up. "Did you get a cabin yet?" I shook my head—mouth full. "Find the chief—El Soldado." I nodded. He rushed out.

Suddenly the mess was empty. The baseball game was loud; it muffled the garbled voices and footsteps scrambling above deck. Then, heavy boots stomped down and into the mess. Black army boots double-laced above the ankles entered and stood in front of me; I chewed.

"Buenas!" a deep voice barked. "I'm the chief mate."

I stood, greeted him, and shook a firm hand. He was taller than I, with bronzed skin and bulging biceps. His black hair was neatly combed back and tied with a band in a tight ponytail. He had the physique of a Greek warrior—Achilles himself. He wore a khaki short sleeve shirt with the first three buttons unfastened. A gold chain disappeared into his hairy chest under a white tank-top. His green fatigue trousers were tucked into his boots. He gestured with two fingers to follow, turned, and marched out. I shoved in a last bite and scrambled humbly behind, chewing. How much had Captain McMorris told him about me? The chief's face revealed nothing.

He marched down the passageway and around the stack to the port side. He stopped in front of the last cabin. "This is yours. Don't worry about working today. You'll need to clean in here. The laundry room's at the far end. The crew does its own wash. I'll send you a pair of coveralls. See Chino, the steward, for linen. We start at six. Breakfast at eight. You'll be chipping rust in the holds 'til we get to Houston—see Rafa, he runs the deck gang."

"Gracias." I shook his hand again and he left.

Holy crap. The room smelled of urine. The bunk was stripped of sheets and the mattress was stained and reeked of piss. The deck was scuffed black from foot traffic and the bulkhead was covered with naked beauties: spread open, bent over, or dangling in bodacious splendor. No shower, only a sink and a toilet. The commode was a dingy yellow, streaked with rust stains, and the sink matched it. I opened the porthole as wide as possible and left the cabin door open.

I raced back to the fourth level and retrieved my suitcase from outside the captain's cabin. Chino gave me a bucket, a scouring pad, some rags, and a full bottle of bleach. I filled the bucket with water in the shower room and turned to. I worked right through dinner. The steward must have felt guilty, for around 1900, he brought some leftover ropa vieja and two bananas with Gordo's blessing.

I used the whole bottle of bleach. At least the cabin smelled clean. But I couldn't get the stains out of the sink or the commode. The bulkhead, deck, mirror, cabinet, closet, and door did improve. I talked the steward out of a brand new mattress along with fresh sheets and towels. Then dogged the porthole open, and latched the door. The bleach smell was strong, but it would evaporate. I unpacked. Later on, lying on my new bunk, I heard a familiar sound—Gordo playing his sad guitar and singing,

> *"Ay Ay Ya Yay*
> *Canta y no llores*
> *Porque cantando se alegran*
> *Cielito lindo, los corazones."*

I stayed awake for several hours listening to his voice boom through the empty passageways from the crew's mess. That song was his motto in life: Sing and be happy for tomorrow you may die.

The darkness crept in and the salty wind gusted through the porthole. I stared at my brother's watch on top of the cabinet and scratched the imprint on my wrist. We'd sail tonight. A new and different day would start tomorrow: the ship, the sea, the crew. I pictured myself jogging on campus again, and talking to the blond with emerald eyes...then I danced with her in my arms and fell asleep.

Chapter 6:
CHIPPING RUST
Holds 1, 2, and 3

A low rumble came up from the deck, pulsated through the bulkhead, and vibrated my bunk. The cabin door rattled against the steel latch that kept it partially opened. Crammed inside the twelve-inch gap, just inside the door on the deck, a pair of leather work gloves lay on top of folded blue coveralls.

I rubbed my eyes, sat up, and dangled my feet a few inches from the deck. The bunk's wooden frame massaged my hamstrings as my legs hung. Lights swayed and moved by the porthole, rather quickly; we were still in the channel. The sky was dark. The city lights were still bright, and veiled the stars. I found my watch—0330. Should try to sleep a couple of hours more. I lay back and curled around my pillow. Images of my brother sinking to the depths crept in. Dad's words sounded in my head. What did I hope to accomplish by sailing out? Then I remembered Sartre's words. "Man can will nothing unless he has first understood that he must count on no one but himself; that he is alone; abandoned on earth." I was abandoned to this choice I'd made—alone at sea.

The first time I'd read those words I'd considered them optimistic and courageous. Now, I felt their sheer hopeless weight. I squeezed the pillow. The easiest thing would've been to accept the loss and move on. Leave it to the Lord, Mom would say. What could I find out? What could I discover that the police and the coast guard could not?

The hum of the engines slowed, then idled. The ship drifted. I hung my head out the porthole. The stars were brighter, city lights now distant. The pilot, dressed in a short-sleeve khaki shirt and shorts, climbed down a rope ladder. A launch came alongside; he let go and dropped in. A few minutes passed and the diesels rumbled again; the low drone returned. *Trader* pitched and swayed. From the open porthole, the warm salty breeze overpowered the bleach. The ocean slapped the hull. I rolled over in my bunk. When I glanced at my watch, an hour had gone by.

Enough self-pity. I sat up and decided to try on my coveralls. I pounced onto the cold deck. The tremors from the powerful engines crept up through my bare feet. I stepped into the coveralls, reached behind for my left sleeve then my right, hoisted them onto my shoulders, and zipped the front halfway up. Perfect fit. I slipped my hands into the gloves and squeezed the fresh leather. My new uniform. Not an officer's. Just a junkyard seaman: a bulldog. I punched my fists together, dropped to the steel and counted off twenty push-ups. I kissed the clean deck each time. I sprang up and boxed the warm air breathing through the porthole. Left, left, left—right cross. Left, left, left—right cross. Left hook—right hook. Left hook—right hook. I rolled one glove over the other like on the speed bag, high stepped right; high stepped left.

I kept this up until sweat moistened the coveralls. I pictured my coach barking orders. What had happened to my brother? Now I was ready for work. Screw this self-pity. My heart pounded in synch with the murmur of the diesels. This was my father's ship, and my ship, too.

Knuckles rapped my door. "Estas listo," Rafa hollered.

"Si." I whipped the gloves off and reached for my old boots, then pulled a sock on each foot, stuck one foot in a boot, then the other. I wrapped the long laces and pulled them tight around my ankles. I stuffed both gloves in a pocket and joined Rafa. He smirked and slapped my shoulder when I came out dressed and sweaty. I followed him down the dark narrow passageway.

A massive steel door led out through the bulkhead of the aft castle to the portside shelter deck. Six feet divided the bulkhead from the bulwark that separated us from the waterline fifty or sixty feet below. The cool wind tossed my long hair and swished by my ears. A faint whiff of fumes from the stack entered my nose. Once the heavy door was dogged shut, the rattle and rumble of the engines subsided to a murmur. The wind flapped our pant legs as we moved forward.

I followed Rafa to the step ladder and down twenty-five or thirty rungs to the main deck. The rungs were wet and slippery, and in the faint light we descended cautiously. The seas were calm and as I climbed down, I looked out toward the open ocean. The moon had disappeared in the west and the only light in the sky was Venus, already high in the east. Low on the eastern horizon, an orange-pink hue divided the sky from the murky sea. With every passing minute, the eastern glow between sea and sky widened far off *Trader*'s port side. The bow pointed south and the empty ship cut through the two-to-three foot chop with ease. Soon she would turn west and pass through the Florida Straits north of Cuba, then head northwest into the Gulf toward Port Houston.

The rungs ended three feet off the portside gunwale. Beyond that, the sea rushed by. On my right, fifteen feet from the bulwark, was No. 6 hold's hatch cover. Centered across the beam, each hold measured forty feet across and close to forty-five feet fore-to-aft, leaving fifteen feet of weather deck on each side. The covers were drawn open and stood over ten feet up on the fore and aft sides of each hold like giant folded tables.

As we walked past No. 5, I gaped into the dark abyss. It dropped belowdeck over forty feet. We walked by three sets of masts, stepped over scuttles to tanks for drinking water, ballast water, fuel oil, and side-stepped mooring cleats for the spring lines. Each double set of mast poles was connected by an elevated platform eight feet above the deck. The platform housed the winch for the booms. Cables were secured to smaller eye-ring cleats along the bulwark. The booms swayed slightly as the ship pitched and rolled, clanging like a brass clip against a flag pole.

At the fore-peak, the deck gang had gathered. They huddled beside several paint buckets filled with chipping hammers, wire brushes, scraping bars, hand brushes, goggles, rags, and small-stuff lines. One sailor carried several shovels and push-brooms on his shoulder. Besides Rafa and me, the deck gang consisted of the three Mexican brothers, the silver-haired pony-tailed carpenter, and the three helmsmen, one of whom was at the wheel and the other, Tomas.

Rafa said everyone was on chipping detail, so the holds could be made ready for loading when we moored at Houston. He tied two half hitches around a paint bucket's handle and drew the hemp tight. Tomas did the same to another. They lowered the tool-laden buckets into No. 1 hold. I followed the Mexicans to the first manhole cover and watched one then another disappear below deck.

I peered into the dark hole. After my eyes adjusted, I saw the ladder welded to the bulkhead and dipped under the cover and took a last glimpse at the sky, now a pale blue. The rungs weren't steps, but round rusted rebar the thickness of a man's thumb. Precarious footing. The steel hand-rail was also rusted and cracked. Without gloves, bloody hands.

As we descended, the chatter between the brothers echoed in the empty cavern. It smelled acrid, moldy, metallic. The deeper into the ship's gut, the heavier the air. Vapors irritated my nostrils and chafed my throat. The dank odors of phosphate and rusted steel permeated the caldron. Below, the corners were still dark. Soon, another line dropped tied to push-brooms and square-point shovels as Spanish bounced about the ship's empty belly like songs in a canyon.

I looked up at the square of dawning sky beyond the gentle oscillation of the mast. The ship moved under my feet like a giant surf board. Through the portside curvature of the inner hull, seawater splashed past. Inside, the hull tapered at about seventy-five degrees and every ten feet angle-iron reinforced the bottom edge of the main deck and connected it with the flat hull we stood on.

The carpenter and the other helmsman groped down the ladder. Rafa and Tomas followed. They had goggles over their eyes and red bandanas tied around mouths and noses. Rafa stood a moment surveying the hold. We gathered around him.

He pulled down his bandana, revealing pockmarked cheeks. "OK, everybody, we're going to concentrate on the worst areas:

angled crevices, rusted-out depressions, and corners where crusted, moist fertilizer has begun to decay the steel. First, brush out the residue. Then, chip out the rust and use the steel brush to leave it ready for red-lead this afternoon. Sweep all the debris to the center. When the pile's large enough, one guy can fill buckets while another goes topside to heave them up and pitch the crap over the side. Clear?"

"Si, Rafa." The group nodded, grunted, and began reaching for tools. Everyone put on goggles, and tied rags or bandanas around his face. The youngest Mexican wrapped an extra shirt around his head and tied a large knot behind; he looked like an Arab. I'd forgotten to bring a bandana, so I took off the t-shirt under my coveralls, ripped it and tied it around my face.

Soon the thunder of hammers echoed like a line-gang beating spikes into railroad ties. The air turned into an orange dusty cloud impossible to breathe without the shirt over my face. My arms, wrists, and face itched, not only from the dust, but also from rust bits and fertilizer particles that shot up at each stroke of my hammer. Chips bounced off my goggles, landed under my collar, into my ears, and filled the tops of my boots. The gritty fumes tasted like the dust from dried battery acid.

I started to sweat. Clumps of rusted metal coated with fertilizer residue burned my skin. I wiped and scratched incessantly. I remembered Tomas telling me how the ship had ulcers. He wasn't joking. We were cleaning the big girl's belly. Like Aesop's slave who'd pulled the thorn from the lion's paw. The lion had repaid the slave. Would *Trader* repay me with the answers I sought?

An hour passed. The sun's light streamed into the orange haze, and the once cool cavern became a steaming oven. The shirt around my face was as brown as a cardboard box. My right arm trembled. Fertilizer tufts dissolved into my sweaty skin. I wiped my goggles. The air was thick as fog.

A few minutes before eight, everyone stopped, dropped tools, and scrambled up the ladder for breakfast. Topside, the cool breeze hit my face like a splash of cold water. Even the skin under my coveralls felt refreshed. I removed the crusted goggles and wiped chips from my cheeks, shook out my hair, blew my nose, coughed and spat. Saliva tasted metallic and granular.

But the sky was bright blue with drifting white puffs scattered high above; the sea a dark blue with white crests breaking. The pounding of hammers was replaced with the rushing wind and waves breaking against the ram-bow. As I walked aft, the ship skated forward under my stride. Flying fish sprang out along the bow, scurried the surface forty or fifty feet, then disappeared under carpets of yellow kelp.

Breakfast was a hectic affair. Everyone rushed, scooped, and inhaled his meal. We had white rice, of course, eggs, potatoes, toast, juice (apple, orange, or grapefruit), bacon or ham, and coffee. No one lingered or joked. Few even washed. They raced to eat as much as possible. Only the basics: eat, piss, shit, and back out on deck until everyone finished. There, a few lit cigarettes: Camels and Lucky Strikes.

At the far end of the after-deck, the Mexicans passed a joint. The big one glared my way then bumped his chin at me. His dark eyes were like a shark's. He'd pulled out his arms from the sleeves of his coveralls. A weightlifting belt kept them from falling off his hips. His sleeveless shirt revealed bronzed and chiseled muscles covered with street-gang ink. Under his left eye was a five-inch gash. He took the last drag and gazed into my eyes, then calmly threw the speck into the sea. I met his scarred stare, but said nothing, turned, and moved down the rungs to the main deck.

I wondered how Roby had meshed with that gang-like Mexican. But my father had been captain then. The Mexican would've stayed clear of the captain's son. He sure had stared at me, though. But he couldn't know who I was; Gordo was a man of his word.

I gawked at the bright morning as I descended the ladder. Flying fish still fluttered from *Trader*'s wake. Leaning on the gunwales, I noticed a parade of seagulls trailing. Gordo dumped breakfast scraps. I stretched to watch. Gulls dive-bombed the surface a hundred yards astern. Sometimes, a pair landed, fought and picked at something, flapped out of the sea, soared up and up, and then dove straight down again. The scene repeated itself until the dumping ceased. They followed the ship from high above, riding the thermals and cawing incessantly. At intervals, one turned, seized the wind, and coasted two or three hundred yards, spying the foamy trail astern. Then it soared up again and effortlessly rejoined the screeching flock of scavengers floating above *Trader*'s aft deck.

Rafa, Tomas, and the carpenter leaned against the coaming to No. 1 hold. Rafa and Tomas drank coffee from Styrofoam cups. The carpenter smoked a cigarette. The sun was hot, but the cool rushing breeze relaxed me, even more with a full stomach. I walked past the gang and went down first this time. It was important to prove myself to these salts. They'd probably been at sea most of their lives. I surveyed the white-capped sea and the open blue sky before I scaled down. It wasn't even 0900 yet. Eleven-thirty was a long, tough, sweat-drenched time away.

Below, I found a push-broom and began piling the chipped debris toward the center. I glanced at the ladder as I worked.

The three Mexicans came down first. Rafa and Tomas stayed topside as the carpenter slowly descended. The big Mexican stopped in front of my push-broom and blocked the path. His younger brothers flanked my sides, no longer friendly and simple-minded as they'd seemed yesterday in the mess.

"Hey, amigo. What's your name again?" He put his left boot on the push-broom.

"Cesar, and you're in my fucking way."

"Ay-ya-ya-ee—he's a tough guy. I'm Coño." In Spanish, Coño means "the bastard" or "hell-bent."

"Listen, I don't give a shit if you smoke weed. So, don't get your panties all bunched up."

He smiled revealing a chipped front tooth. His younger brothers slapped hands and banged fists together. They were giddy; eyes blood-shot and squinty.

The carpenter planted his feet, turned from the ladder, and saw us. "Let's go, cabrones."

Coño took his boot off my broom. "That's OK; you and I'll talk again." I met his eyes, said nothing, and nodded. Now I had one Mexican friend—Gordo, and three Mexican foes—Coño and his brothers.

The pounding, chipping, scraping, brushing, and shoveling took up the rest of the morning. The orange cloud returned. Buckets filled with debris dangled up, and Tomas dumped the contents overboard. About an hour before lunch, Rafa yelled down to Coño and his brothers to get started in No. 2. The three eyeballed me before starting the climb. Coño pointed and smirked. I nodded again.

The carpenter watched. "I see you made some friends." He grinned.

43

"They were abused children." I said. He laughed and kept chipping rust. I filled buckets with crud.

Lunch time brought a feast: pork chops, mashed potatoes with gravy, yuca, and the usual—white rice. I ate two full servings and washed it down with apple juice. After lunch, the Mexicans smoked another joint by the bulwark. They made no bones to hide it. I wondered if the chief mate knew, if my father knew. On the walk back, I decided to find out.

I caught up with Tomas in front of No. 2. He smoked a cigarette and leaned on the gunwales. He stared out at the sea. The day remained clear, hot, and windy. *Trader* pitched and heaved more; the waves had increased. Four-to-five foot rollers slammed the starboard side and sprayed the deck.

"Hey, Tomas, you smoke, too."

"Si—why, you want a cigarette?"

"No, I mean weed."

"Sometimes. You're from Miami, right? Don't tell me you haven't burned one before."

"Sure. But doesn't the chief check on that?"

"You mean 'cause he's a soldier and all? Hell, he does worse."

"What do you mean?"

"Don't ask too much. Just do your work. OK?"

"Sure, man." I left it at that. I didn't want a fourth enemy. He scowled, flicked the butt into a comber, turned his back, and marched off.

That stifled conversation for the rest of the afternoon. We banged out the No. 2 hold and then No. 3 until the sun began to ease off its scorching torture. We didn't have time for red-lead before six and left it for the next morning.

I had to wash my hands and face before dinner. I reeked of sweat. My face was covered with rust particles; the dirt left the imprint of the goggles around my eyes. My ears had crap in them, so did my hair and neck line. I wanted a shower, but I wanted food first. I sat next to the carpenter during chow. We had salad, picadillo, fried plantains, and, naturally, white rice. Again I ate two heaping servings, washed it down with apple juice and then hit the shower room. The showers were shared by the crew; the officers had their own. At sea, in the shower-room, the water flowed from 1800 to 2000 and from 0400 to 0600. If you missed those times, you were screwed.

After a hot shower, I plunked down in my bunk like an old hound after a long hunt. If Gordo strummed his sad songs I didn't hear them. The cool salty breeze rushed in my porthole and *Trader* rocked me to sleep.

Chapter 7:
CHIPPING RUST
Holds 4, 5, and 6

I woke a second before hands, knees, and elbows slammed the deck. *Trader*, fighting rougher seas, had pitched me from the bunk. I lay on my side, rubbed my knees and grinned.

The wind howled and whistled through the porthole. Then the smile receded. Coño and his brothers. I'd avoided them yesterday after dinner, but he'd brush me today for sure. I'd best get ready.

I stumbled to my feet, massaged my elbows and checked the time, 0457. Early waking—a blessing from the *Trader*? I boxed the air, did push-ups, sit-ups and worked up a sweat. The tattooed Mexican had probably stewed and schemed all night. He'd try to corner me inside one of the holds. He was king of the deck gang and I'd shot him down in front of his brothers. He'd never let that slide. I wouldn't be able to count on anything or anyone. I was alone. I remembered Dad's warning when he'd slapped my face at Port Everglade. "Don't drop your guard."

Yesterday's sweat, orange dust, and paint chips still saturated my coveralls. I shook them out then on again, over a clean t-shirt, underwear, and socks. I brushed my teeth and washed my face. Knuckles rapped twice, followed by a hissing whistle. Heavy footsteps faded down the passageway. It was time.

I put on ankle braces over my socks, laced the boots through every eyelet, pulled the strings twice around the top, and yanked down tight like a bowline on a bight. Jumped around a little to ease the tension. Slipped on the wrist braces under each work glove. Closed the door and started down the black heaving passageway.

The heavy steel bulkhead door flung open in the wet salty wind after I hammered the dog-latch open with a fist. It bounced off the bulkhead and swivelled back on well-greased hinges. I fought it closed and dogged it.

Ten feet of spray engulfed the fo'c'sle like a foamy blanket. The white splash stood out against the dark deck in the faint dawn light. The mast lights, still on, cast shifting shadows on the hatch covers halfway shut to block the rain and spray. Thin films of seawater flooded and streamed along the deck. When the ship rolled, the foamy water sought scuppers and disappeared. The wind-spray stung my face and eyes like rock-salt fired from a twelve-gauge. My hair tossed about; my pants legs slapped with the wind. Before reaching the ladder to the main deck, I was drenched. Hadn't eaten breakfast yet, and already I tasted salt water. It bit my otherwise dry throat.

With a tight grip on the handrails, I scaled down the ladder, my back to the deck. Without a horizon, the dark sky blended into the dark ocean. The only distinguishable difference—whitecaps. The deck was slippery. I steadied myself against the bulwarks as I moved toward No. 4 hold. The ram-bow slammed into a wave; *Trader* vibrated then dropped into the trough. Moments later, she pitched up again. I stopped several times and braced, waited for the bow to drop, shuffled forward eight or nine feet, and braced again. Ten-to-twelve foot rollers tossed and rumbled the empty ship. She was like a truck without shock absorbers bouncing on a rocky road.

The helmsman named Simon, the carpenter, and Rafa crouched underneath the winch's platform between No. 3 and No. 4. The carpenter had pulled a jacket over his head to screen off the wind and smoke a cigarette. They sipped coffee from Styrofoam cups. Paint buckets filled with tools, brooms, and shovels shifted between them. I glanced aft. Coño and his brothers came pussyfooting along the deck. The rags tied over their heads flapped in the wind. Each held one arm in front of his eyes to block the stinging spray; the other hand clutched the gunwales.

As they crossed the deck, Coño leaned into one of his brothers and shoved him into me. I smashed into Rafa as he crouched against the coaming to No. 4. My knee knocked the coffee out of his hand. He jumped up. "Puta madre," he growled. I reared back with a forearm across the chest of the skinny kid, Lupe. Coño caught his brother and glared. Coño was a few inches taller than his younger brothers but I was two inches taller than he.

"All right! Enough bullshit, you three," Rafa grunted and watched the wind take the empty cup far over the side. It danced along the waves and disappeared. "You four start here in No. 4." He pointed to me and the Mexicans. "And we'll start with red-lead in No. 1 and 2. Tomas'll join us after lunch. He's sleeping; was at the wheel late. El Indio'll be at the helm all day. So, we've got to move."

El Indio was from Guatemala and I'd heard was the best helmsman aboard. Simon, dark and also Indian-looking, came from Nicaragua. Tomas, I already knew, came from Maracaibo, Venezuela. Tomas had told me Rafa had been born in Spain, but had grown up in Argentina. Rafa's father, also a merchant sailor, had moved his family to La Plata, near Buenos Aires, when Rafa was a child. The carpenter didn't reveal much.

Simon and the carpenter staggered off toward the fore-peak to get brushes and red-lead. Rafa started lowering the tools as the Mexicans and I climbed down into No. 4. I followed Lupe into the manhole. Coño and the other youngster named Enrique came next. I felt like a prisoner scourged into a dungeon. The damp dusty vapors in the cool chamber filled my lungs. The darkness was ominous with the hatch covers half closed. The cavern echoed a loud thud each time one of us jumped off the ladder. It carried like a bass drum in an army band.

Rafa lowered the bucket of tools. It swung like a pendulum as the ship heaved, then crashed and spilled chipping hammers, scraping bars, and wire brushes on the deck. A second line with brooms and shovels swayed down. He positioned a spotlight at one corner of the hatch cover, tied it off, and plugged it in. He angled it toward one side. "Start there." Rafa yelled from above. "When the sun comes up, maybe we won't need the lamp." The light revealed the cave's corners like headlights through an alley.

Coño stood in the shadow of the hatch beam. He waited until Rafa left. Enrique stood to his right and let Coño speak around him. "I told you we'd talk again, amigo."

Lupe flanked my left side and inched around. I shuffled back to keep my left eye on Lupe. "Kinda lonely down here—right?" Coño lurched a half a step forward. I took a basic stance and pointed my left toe at his front foot. My knees bent, right foot up on my right toe, arms up, elbows in, head turtled in between both fists. I swayed as the ship pitched.

49

"So you think what . . . you some kinda fighter?" His tone was low, from the throat. He flicked his right hand as he spoke. His neck muscles flexed as he stuck out his lower jaw. He talked through clenched teeth, cocked his head, and stared into my eyes. He moved closer. From my left, Lupe crept in. The range shrank. The ship rocked. The light tilted. The moment flashed like a Saturday night brawl. The Mexicans surrounded me like wolves.

Suddenly, Lupe dove at the back of my legs. The moment I glanced down, Coño hurled a wild overhand right. I stepped back, ducked in the shell of my arms, and blocked the punch with my left forearm, but fell over the runt and landed on my ass. As Lupe tried to get up, I kicked him flush in the nose. Coño shoved him out of the way and jumped on top of me. His first punch hit my ribs. I cringed from the impact. I blocked his second and third wild hooks, sat up, and head-butted him on the forehead as his gut landed against my knees. My teeth ground with the jolt. The collision stunned him. I was dazed, too.

Enrique ran full stride from behind Coño with a chipping hammer in his right hand. I curled up like a shrimp on a hook. The blow struck my thigh. I yelled, rolled over and away. His second swing missed and glanced off the bare steel deck with a reddish spark in the gloomy darkness. I rolled again. As he reared back for a third strike, I jumped up on one leg. He flung the hammer at my face. I stuck my left hand out and the heavy tool smashed into my knuckles and caromed over my arm. The handle struck my mouth and split my lip. I staggered back against the bulkhead and hunched over. My lip swelled and bled. I stood bewildered.

Coño raged by Enrique and with two long strides was on me again. I hopped back and hunched down in my shell-like stance and stopped a wild hook with my forearm. He followed it with a right to my solar plexus. My lungs collapsed and I crumbled to the deck. I couldn't breathe. I lay on my left side with my back against the bulkhead. He took a few steps back waited for the ship to roll, and came at me again. I peered at him with one eye, face pressed against the rough rusty deck. He shifted his weight to his right foot, then his left and balanced himself to kick me in the face. As he reared back his boot, I kicked back the knee of the leg he stood on. It snapped, so loud it echoed. He fell backward, clutching the knee with both hands, and let out a bloodcurdling scream. "Cabron! Te voy a matar! Te voy a matar!" I still couldn't get up; my lungs were pancaked, airless. Enrique took one knee next to Coño waiting for orders. Lupe winced on the deck, holding his bloody nose.

"What the hell is going on down there?" Rafa's holler echoed down into the dungeon. "Cesar, get your ass up here and go brush lead up front. Send Simon back here to No. 4. Hurry up!"

I sprang to my feet. Lupe held his bloody nose. Coño held his knee with both hands; his face red, anguished. His veins bulged. I limped past him toward the ladder. My ribs ached; my lip was swollen and my left thigh throbbed.

Mounting the ladder was a slow process. One rung at a time, I gripped the rusted steel with scraped and swollen knuckles. My left thigh twitched as I shifted my weight onto that leg. My ribs twinged when I reached for each rung and pulled. I snailed upward.

Topside, a red dawn. The fresh breeze left me faint from the climb. I leaned against the hatch's coaming. *Trader* plunged through a wave; I relaxed in safety.

51

The rest of the morning trickled by without further incident. The carpenter and I brushed red-lead over chipped-out cavities. The work soothed my spirit and numbed the pain. The sun came up just before breakfast and the wind died back considerably. The ship still keeled and lurched through the ocean, but the squall passed, and the rollers decreased to about five to six feet.

Breakfast turned into a stare-down contest. Coño sat on the bench with his knee wrapped and glared at me. The kids gawked. I studied their faces. Lupe kept blotting his nose with a paper napkin. I had a knot on my forehead and a swollen hand. My thigh and ribs throbbed. Coño also sported a red lump on his forehead. He'd probably cool it for today.

And he did. They smoked their ritual joint after breakfast. Apparently, Coño's leg wasn't broken, but he limped. He leaned against the bulwark keeping weight off it. I avoided eye contact and went up to the bow with the carpenter. We finished No. 3 by lunchtime. The Mexicans and Simon had No. 4 done and most of No. 5 chipped out. The sun shone bright and hot.

For chow, Gordo cooked pork chops, mashed potatoes, plantains and the usual white rice. I ate like an escaped prisoner. Afterwards, the Mexican gang huddled aft by the bulwark once more. I started to wonder how much weed they had.

On the way back from lunch, I stopped and leaned on the gunwale to feel the breeze. White-caps were everywhere. Clouds sprinkled across a gray-blue sky. Directly in front of me, thirty or forty yards from the ship, two, three…five shiny gray silhouettes streaked by towards the bow, dolphins. I wobbled to the fo'c'sle and stuck my head into the thru-hull for the bow line. Tail-fins beat the surface as they submarined from side to side over the top edge of the ram-bow. They propelled along lunging and diving. Every so often one would break the surface and out popped a foamy steam as the blow-hole opened with an audible puff. The sideshow lasted for a time and then, as though a whistle had blown, they disappeared.

The day dragged. The afternoon sun beat down. The work paced on. The ship swayed and pitched. Waves beat the rambow. The wind brought salty spray. Seagulls came and went. A pair of frigate birds followed for a time framed high above the masts by the cargo hold. Tomas joined the chipping gang around 1300. Simon left for the wheelhouse at 1600. The carpenter and I finished brushing No. 5 with red-lead before 1800 leaving No. 6 chipped out, but without lead.

At dinner Tomas sat beside me. "Heard you fought Coño and his brothers." He studied the lump on my head and swollen lip.

"Yeah, but Rafa stopped it before things got out of hand."

"Tienes huevos." He raised his thumb. For someone to stand up to Coño apparently required balls. Tomas stared into my eyes for a moment, then nodded. "We'll get to Houston by 0500, you know."

"Really?"

"Yeah, and set sail before the next morning. American ports work fast. And then, Venezuela y muchas niñas lindas." He raised both eyebrows.

I hit the showers first again. My bunk was a welcome sight. Around 2030, I heard Gordo's voice and guitar serenade the empty passageways again.

"Yo soy un hombre sincero.
De donde crece la palma.
Y antes de morir quiero.

53

Echar mis versos del alma.
Guantanamera Guajira Guantanamera.
Guantanamera Guajira Guantanamera"

Guess he'd heard about the fight. I checked Roby's watch. The crystal was cracked. Once again the salty wind rushed in my porthole. I was a worn out sailor, bruised but still here.

8:
PORT HOUSTON

I woke just before 0500. The engines had changed from the pounding thud-rhythm to a low, damped rumble. I sprang up and looked out my porthole. Lights dotted a misty shoreline. *Trader* was coasting into Galveston Bay. A blinking amber light centered above a red and a green approached through the haze. The pilot's launch slowly appeared out of the smog. I stuck my head out the porthole. Muddled voices shouted back and forth on the main deck. The small craft cut back its throttle and came alongside. It pitched and rolled in *Trader*'s wake.

From the gunwales a rope-ladder unfurled to the waterline. *Trader* lost her way and drifted. The launch matched her speed. Swells of foam rolled from the stern. A sailor inside the launch grabbed the rope-ladder and heaved it taut. A stout pilot, dressed in white and wearing a white navy-like peaked cap, struggled with his grip. He found his footing on the second wooden rung, knocked against the hull, and climbed up. Hands and arms helped him over the gunwales. Pilot aboard, the launch roared away and disappeared into the murky distance. Up came the rope ladder. Minutes later, the diesels rumbled and the pulsating beat returned. She was underway again—headed for the Houston Ship Channel.

Landfall, the jagged skyline above the coast, lifted my spirits. My swollen hand and lip, my bruised thigh and ribs hurt less than yesterday. I checked the time on Roby's watch. Grimy coveralls lay on the deck. I dressed and stared through the porthole at the morning's dark sky.

I hadn't forgotten why I'd shipped out. But what had I learned so far? Gordo knew nothing. The Mexican gang led by Coño had plenty of weed on board and openly smoked every day. And Tomas had hinted at something about the chief. Along with almost getting killed in the hold, that's all I knew. Not very substantial. Sartre's themes echoed: Nothingness, Abandoned, Alone, Ultimate Responsibility. Coño had it in for me now. Should I give up? Jump ship in Houston and go home? Venezuela was a long way from safety. Coño might try again. Could he've killed Roby? Dad had been the captain at the time. But the chief mate really ran operations. Everyone answered to the chief before the captain. Coño answered to the chief.

Knuckles rapped the door. The carpenter stood outside. "Gordo made breakfast early today. Pilot's on board. We'll be docking around 0800." I followed him down the passageway, around the stack to the starboard side, and into the mess.

Rafa, the Mexicans, two helmsmen, and the oilers sat inside scarfing down breakfast: just eggs, bacon, juice, and coffee. Lupe complained. "No hay arroz?" Coño's scowl followed me. I shoveled eggs onto my plate and sat with the carpenter and Tomas.

Heavy boots stormed down the ladderway. The chief marched in, dressed in a khaki shirt neatly tucked into green fatigues tucked into black army boots. The mess grew silent. He turned to the boatswain. "Rafa, forget brushing lead in No 6. We'll load it like it is." Rafa nodded and the chief continued. "As soon as we're secure we'll start loading No 1. Two teams for mooring. The second engineer will go with Coño and his brothers aft. Rafa, Cesar, and the carpenter on the fo'c'sle with me. The third mate will stay midship and join Tomas and Simon to secure the gangplank and make ready. The second mate will be on the bridge with the captain and the pilot."

Low mutters filled the mess.

"Now, I've had a report of some bullshit going on!" He glared at me. His bronzed skin contrasted with his light tan shirt; biceps bulged against the short sleeves; his black hair was neatly tied in a ponytail. "That ends today—understood?" He stared at me and waited for a response. I nodded. I couldn't believe he was taking Coño's side. I wanted to say something, but kept quiet. Had Captain McMorris told him who I was?

"Now as soon as everyone's eaten, report to your station. Tidy the decks. We'll be tying up on the starboard side. Lash monkey-fist heave lines to the bight of the hawsers for the bow and stern lines, and the cross and quarter springs. Have the breast hawsers ready, but we may not use them if the channel's calm. And have spikes and stopper-lines ready." He glanced at Rafa, then at Coño. One nodded; the other grunted. "When we tie up, I want no slack from the winches to the bitts. Got that, Coño?" Coño started to say something but groaned instead. The chief carried on. "The pilot will signal me by radio when to pass to the dock. When the gangway's secure, let's roll back all the hatch covers we're scheduled to start loading as soon as we spot No. 1 under the conveyor belt. Any questions?"

Everyone shook his head. The soldier searched everyone's eyes and paused again when he looked at me. He turned and disappeared; boots thumped up the ladderway.

By 0630 everyone piled out of the mess. I followed Rafa and the carpenter forward through the shelter deck and down the ladder to the main deck. The air was crisp like a cool autumn night. Coastal lights glittered on the horizon. A 747 thundered overhead. Just beyond the bow, the Baytown Bridge came into view. It joined southwest Baytown, Texas to northeast La Porte. The cable-stayed bridge towered almost 200 feet from the waterline and stood half as wide as a football field. I gaped up as *Trader* churned beneath, my mouth wide, skin tingling, mind blank. In the distance, white stacks and silos clustered along the shoreline of San Jacinto Bay.

Rafa went down to the forepeak. The carpenter and I followed. The chief, El Soldado as everyone called him, went up to the fo'c'sle, eyes forward, and waited for us to return.

The forepeak, the deck compartment below the fo'c'sle, was the storehouse for deck tools and tackle. We entered through a steel hatchway and stepped over the shin-high coaming. Inside, the carpenter, a tall man, ducked to clear rusty blocks hanging from the overhead. The air was cold and musty with the odors of linseed paint, oils, and sweet hemp fiber that reminded me of the marijuana the Mexicans had been smoking.

On the left, coils of lines were piled chest high: hawsers as thick as Captain McMorris's calves, small-stuff like messenger and kite lines, rusty wire, cable, and chains with links the size of coconuts. On the right, rough pine crates were heaped with shackles, hooks, links, and spikes, wire cutters and bolt cutters, come-alongs and assorted blocks, paint brushes and wire brushes with chipping hammers, carpentry hammers and sledge hammers; brooms, rakes, spades, shovels and Johnson bars. The crates were corralled by a frame of 2x4s. Standing in a corner was a pile of small and medium sized anchors: grapnels for dragging, mooring clumps for buoys, and two Danforths for muddy or sandy bottoms. A spare ship anchor was lashed into place awaiting its turn to one day touch bottom.

Other crates held parts for the windlass, winches, booms, hatch covers, gangplanks and rope-ladders. Brightly colored plastic milk crates filled with mason jars had nails, screws, nuts and bolts, wire clips and rope clips, grommets and wire, grease and lubricants. Behind the crates, stacked on the deck was wood for dunnage. And on the deck, against the bulkhead with a 2x10 enclosing the front, were rows of five-gallon paint and red-lead cans. On both sides of the entrance way against the bulkhead were industrial-size drums of navy blue paint, red-lead, hydraulic oil and bearing grease. The drums were secured with 2x10s jammed against the drums and screwed into 2x4s scabbed onto the bulkhead.

Rafa grabbed several monkey-fist lines and hemp stoppers that lay coiled and piled inside a wooden crate. He handed me three and slipped the others through his arms onto his shoulder. I did the same. The carpenter picked up marlinspikes and a five-pound sledge hammer from another large crate filled with hooks and links, chains and shackles.

As I emerged from below deck, the bright dawn glazed the Baytown horizon in a pink hue off the starboard side. Off to port, the battleship *Texas* lay dingy-gray and abandoned. Again I stared—Tabula Rasa—and my senses tingled. My eyes were wide open, my throat dry, nostrils inhaling the salty air, ears ready for orders but aware of the wind rushing by, my hands snug in my gloves and gripping rough twine, boots tied tight as I stood balanced on the fo'c'sle. *Trader* pushed on through Channelview and west into the Houston Channel.

Not far ahead, a massive bow approached with only two lighted masts—*Texas Star*. The monstrous tanker glided by seventy-five feet off our port side. Sailors gave us the finger from the port wing and smiled. Oil refineries dotted the landscape behind her spewing smog and long cotton trails of white steam from their stacks.

"Cesar, put down those lines and help me fake down the spring line," Rafa snapped as I gawked at the tanker and returned the finger at the sailors on her afterdeck. The chief stood by the portside bitts watching. The carpenter reeved one monkey-fist line by the starboard thru-hull and began lashing it to the bight of the bow-spring line as Rafa and I faked the hawser out in front of the winches. Then we faked down the forward breast-line by the starboard bulwarks and reeved the second monkey-fist line by the thru-hull and lashed it to the bight of the bow line on the port side. We flemished each lead line next to the bight of each hawser, leaving them neatly coiled, with the monkey-fist in the center ready to pass to the line-handlers.

Next, Rafa picked up a control box on a cable and tested each winch by starting them and giving the gypsy head a revolution. Each clicked, geared up smartly, and he shut them down. He nodded at the chief. I handed Rafa the stopper lines and he set them on the deck, one by each winch with a marlinspike inside the coil.

I looked up. The next bridge was growing just ahead—the Sam Houston Ship Channel Bridge. It had nearly the same clearance as the Baytown Bridge but the width bottlenecked to around seventy feet. Each side had a white pelican gracing the top of a piling. They watched our ship glide by as if guarding the channel.

Steering alongside other vessels required more precision now. I glanced back at the bridge. El Indio was at the helm. Boats passed alongside heading out: a Boston Whaler with a father at the wheel and two teenagers sitting on the deck rigging bait; a thirty foot Grady White with a flying bridge and outriggers; a Dusky trolling the channel—probably for tarpon; a 65 foot Bertram crowded with silver haired couples already drinking—most likely chartered; a shrimp boat with nets furled and stacked with lobster traps fore and aft with a flock of screaming gulls in close pursuit. *Trader* continued west as the channel widened after the bridge. Gulls, terns, skimmers, and pelicans thronged the air over the waterway. A trio of frigate birds soared high above, keeping pace with the shrimp boat. The rising sun perched for a moment framed through the clearance of the Sam Houston Bridge, now a mile astern.

El Soldado moved to the point of the bow and stood with legs apart, arms folded, short black ponytail unaffected by the wind. He stared forward like a Viking ready for battle. I studied him. His presence. His posturing. This was his ship. He'd been on the bridge when Roby went overboard. That son of a bitch knew more than was he saying.

I glared at him—the bronzed statue in control of the ship. I gritted my teeth. I flexed my jaw and neck muscles the way Coño had just before I fought him inside the hold. I squeezed my fists inside my gloves and pictured myself in front of the heavy bag with my boxing coach barking at me. Left—left—right. Left—left—right.

"Cesar, what the fuck you doing, hombre?" Rafa snapped again. The chief mate turned. I dropped my head and moved beside Rafa.

A third bridge appeared around a bend in the channel. The Sidney Sherman was a low bridge. Dad had told me he'd seen a tanker collide with the struts when she veered from the center of the waterway. I looked for the scarred struts as we passed under.

I tried to focus on my work, but remained obsessed with analyzing the chief. Why would he take Coño's side? What the fuck was that about? I began to curse more when I talked to myself—when I thought of Roby—when I thought of Coño—and now, when I thought of the chief, El Soldado. I scowled each time I thought of them. My stare and clenched jaw harnessed a caged beast. I tried to veil my suspicions about Roby's death.

Finally, the port of Houston came into view. The mooring process went by in a mental fog. I was barely cognizant of my surroundings. A tugboat honked, nearly deafening us. The pier had a curtain of old tires stretched from bollard to bollard like black, curly-bearded smiles. A row of pelicans and cormorants roosted at the far end of the pier primping and ruffling their wings. The engines stopped. Instructions squawked back and forth on the hand held radio as the tug nudged us into our berth. Rafa passed the monkey-fist line for the cross-spring hawser to the linesmen on the pier. The line ran out. The tug braked her forward surge. The linesmen hauled the dropped hawsers up from the dirty river. Linesmen slipped the bight of the hawser around a bollard. The tug rumbled, spewed diesel smoke, bubbled and shot up green river water from its stern. *Trader* swayed. The carpenter passed the monkey-fist line for the bow line to the dock. That hawser ran out. Rafa wrapped the cross-spring line three times around the drum to the starboard winch. I helped the carpenter carry the bow line to one of the gypsy heads on the windlass. The radio squawked again. The winch hummed and rotated, hauling in the spring line. The stern winch hauled in the quarter-spring. The bow and stern lines lay slack in the water. Then the radio squawked again. The carpenter kicked on the gypsy head. The tug moved in across the port-side beam and the ship nudged the tires. I wrapped and tightened a stopper-line around the hawsers near the bitts and pulled off the slacked line from the drum. Lines slackened to the dock. The chief yelled. We wrapped each hawser three times around the foot of the bitts, let go of stopper-lines, and reeved figure eights around the bitts. A few more turns from the winches and she touched the tires again.

A white car pulled up alongside the beam. The door read Texas Port Authority. The gangplank began descending from the davit of the main deck. She was secure and ready to load beneath the massive railway that held the conveyor belt. At the end of the belt, a giant grain chute aimed its maw down at us. The tug thundered off. I stared at the chief as he marched off the fo'c'sle to the gangway, greeted each of the authorities with a firm hand shake, and led the way up the ladder to the captain's cabin.

Rafa ordered the carpenter and me to start rolling back No 1's hatch cover. The massive steel railway girders above the ship engaged with a clang, and the chute rolled and squeaked into position above the center of No. 1. High above, through the windows of the station, a blond-bearded man in a seersucker engineer cap watched us work. A fat black man in a white short sleeve shirt held a two-way radio and waited.

The hatch covers squeaked and rumbled open. As the wedge batten rolled back on steel wheels, the hatch beam ran into the stiffener and the cover parted and folded up rolling to the end of the coaming like a giant folding card table. We left it open and proceeded to No. 2. Midship, the second engineer, in greasy coveralls and with sandy hair dancing in the wind, operated the winch for No. 5 and No 6. The carpenter went to the platform for No. 3 and No. 4. When No. 4's hatch opened, I peered over the coaming at the corner of the hold where I'd battled the Mexicans.

By the time we finished rolling back all the hatch covers, the port authority men appeared on the shelter deck and began descending the ladder to the main deck. One carried a small briefcase; the other a two-way radio. They cordially waved at the third mate and Tomas as they jogged down the gangway. Moments later, the conveyor belt above No. 1 whined and shuddered like a bitch having puppies. A dark, reddish sandy stream poured into No. 1 hold. Brownish-red dust immediately rose up and hovered around the coaming like a sand storm.

We spent the rest of the morning supervising the acrid cargo as it discharged into No. 1 and No. 2. Once those holds were topped off, we climbed down with shovels to trim and level the cone of powdery muddy-red fertilizer. Then we retrieved the 2x8s and the 2x12s from the forepeak. Across the top of the leveled granules, we set two rows of the twenty foot 2x12s into slots along the fore and aft bulkhead of each hold. These would keep the cargo from shifting in rough seas, making us list and maybe even capsize.

During lunch, Rafa and the second engineer stayed on deck supervising the discharge. After their dogwatch, they went to lunch.

We kept loading all afternoon. Once No. 3 and No. 4 filled, we leveled and trimmed back the fertilizer, then secured the partitions. By supper there were only two empty holds. The dock workers thinned out to a skeleton crew and so did we. Flood lights came on, lighting the pier like a giant stadium. The red cloud over *Trader* created a halo as the light reflected off the dust particles. The nimbus gave the *Trader* a spooky appearance as it loaded fertilizer that would grow corn and beans for Venezuela's people.

Sometime after midnight, the holds were full. We rolled the hatch covers back and secured watertight tarpaulins over the holds. Then the ship bunkered fuel, oil, and fresh water. The chandler brought stores and supplies for Gordo. The ship was ready for her voyage across the Gulf.

By 0300 I still hadn't slept. I chose to work overtime—after departure there wouldn't be as much to do. I sat on the fo'c'sle with a cup of stale black coffee and listened to the sound of pumps and engines rumbling from the warehouse. The pier remained illuminated by the giant flood lights.

Around 0400, our engines began to vibrate the deck and bulkheads. A tug appeared and rumbled close astern. Linesmen sauntered out from the warehouse and stood by each bollard, then let go the spring-lines. We hauled them in. Then the linesmen walked to the stern, smoking and talking, and let go those hawsers, leaving only the bow line fast to the dock. The tug came alongside our starboard and nudged us away from the pier. The chief started up the gypsy head to slack the bow line, and the linesmen tossed our line into the river. The windlass reversed and hauled it in. Then the tug nudged our beam until the bow pointed east and our engines engaged with a snort of dark brown smoke from the stack, a whiff of oil and sulphur.

We were underway again, headed for Venezuela. After breakfast, I went to sleep.

9:
GULF OF MEXICO

A fist sledgehammered my door. "Cesar, answer up!"

I scrambled to my feet and opened it, rubbing my eyes. The chief stood in the passageway. "Yes, Chief."

"Captain says you're a decent helmsman. That so?"

"Well...yes sir."

"Simon's asthmatic. Breathing all that fertilizer dust triggered his seizures. I need you at the wheel, third shift."

"When?" I ran my fingers through my hair and scratched the top of my head.

"I know you're signed on as an ordinary seaman, not a certified AB. But we need you anyways. The officers do four hour shifts; the helmsmen eight. So the third shift from 2400 to 0800 is yours until further notice." He pointed a finger. "I'll be there with you." His dark stabbing eyes held no clues; his stiff face no expression.

"Very well, sir." I stared at him puzzled. He nodded and left. I closed my door and checked Roby's watch. Almost time for lunch. I felt cornered. I needed to talk to Gordo. McMorris must have told the chief I was Captain Santino's oldest son. If so, the chief was keeping that to himself. Why? I remembered a line from the movie *The Godfather*—"Keep your friends close, but your enemies closer." And "Women and children can be careless, but not men." I didn't trust this guy. Not one bit. It would only make sense that the chief would have asked McMorris how he knew I was a good helmsman. And then, the captain would have told him who I was. But why didn't he say something about it? He was usually direct. Out of respect for Roby? But he was too quiet. And now, I'd be on watch with him.

I rushed aft through the passageway, around the stack, and leaped down the ladderway, bracing on the handrails and catapulting three steps at once. I wanted to get there before the crew started to eat. As I turned the bottom corner, I saw Gordo's massive body hunched over, just inside the galley. He pulled a long flat pan from the oven.

"Gordo, I have to talk to you." I scrambled past the entranceway to the crew's mess and spied the steward, Chino. He held a water pitcher and had his back to me. I stepped in next to the cook. The galley was hot and muggy. Steam rose from the pots on the stove. A fan in front of the porthole buzzed and circulated the warm air.

"Que te pasa, cabron?" He turned, holding the hot, flat pan of picadillo with a rag in each hand and set it down on the metal countertop across from the oven. His oily face dripped beads of sweat. He wiped it with his greasy apron. The rich saucy odor of ground beef seasoned with red peppers and onions rose with the hot steam. My stomach gurgled. The fan hummed behind us in a half-moon dance.

"The chief ordered me to steer on third shift."

Gordo kept working and listened. I watched and waited for a response. He covered the pan of meat with aluminum foil and slid it to the end of the countertop ready for the steward. After that, he stirred a giant crock-pot of rice, and then started cutting up plantains to fry. He paused from slicing and looked up. "So—good for you. Maybe that'll keep you and Coño apart."

"Hey, let me ask you—is Coño the chief's enforcer, or something?

"What?"

"Yeah, you heard me. Are they friends? Does he do his bidding?"

"Everyone does what the Soldier says. He's damn tough. He runs things. Look—just do your work and keep quiet."

"Bullshit, Gordo. Coño and his brothers tried to kill me for no reason. And the chief took his side yesterday. He has to know what really happened in the hold with Coño. And how 'bout Roby?" Gordo stopped working and stared at me with his mouth open. He studied my angry face and my clenched fists. He took a step back. I moved closer; my face only a few inches from his. "Did you forget about him? Did you? The chief was on the bridge that morning—remember."

"Suave, man . . . suave. You're right . . . but I really don't know about Coño and the chief," he said, holding up both hands and shaking his head. Then he wiped his face from the spray of my words.

"Bullshit, Gordo—Bullshit! I don't believe you." He was scared. He was actually scared. Of me?—or my questions? I spun around and stormed out of the galley.

Chino stood at the entrance to the crew's mess, watching and listening. I cut in front of him. He dropped his head, moved into the galley, and continued his chores. I sat at the table closest to the entranceway with the bulkhead at my back and a full view of the mess room. Chino returned with a large bowl of white rice in each hand and set one at the head of both tables. The other messman followed with two casserole dishes of picadillo and put one by each rice bowl. Then Chino came back with bowls of fried plantains. I thanked him—an apology.

A long, cool gulp from a tall glass of ice water soothed my dry throat. I had to calm down. The first sentence of the Desiderata: "Go placidly amid the noise and haste, and remember what peace there may be in silence." That's it—silence. Stay calm. Stay quiet at the wheel tonight. Let the chief talk. Watch him. Study him. Like a chess match. But this was no game.

Footsteps clamored down the ladderway. Lupe and Enrique stepped in pushing and jabbing at each other's dusty coveralls. Shirt rags were still tied around their heads. They entered, noticed me, and froze for a moment, then moved cautiously by, like dogs staying clear of a panther.

Coño followed. He hobbled in with a brace on his knee over his jeans and wearing a sleeveless shirt. He stared at me, defiant as an injured wolf. He leaned on my table as he went by and flexed the ink on his left triceps. The gang of three sat at the second table facing me. Coño turned sideways on the end of the bench. He stretched his right leg out in the aisle, balanced by his right elbow on the table. Lupe smiled at me, lifted his chin, and with the thumb of his left fist, slowly gestured a slice across his throat. His eyes opened wild and wide as he glared. I picked up a paper napkin, pretended to blot my nose, and smiled back. His nose was dark and swollen.

Rafa and Tomas came in and dropped across from me. Rafa purposely blocked my sight of the Mexicans. "Haven't you had enough yet?" He raised his eyebrows and bumped his chin at me. I met his gaze until he glanced away.

"Chief talked to you yet?" Tomas grabbed the water pitcher and filled his glass.

"Yeah, I'm at the wheel third shift."

"I'll be on the bridge at 1600," Tomas said, and passed Rafa the pitcher.

"You're still on the deck till 1800," Rafa jabbed back and filled his glass.

"Yeah, I figured as much," I countered, and held my glass out so he'd refill it. He smirked.

The carpenter walked in. His tool belt sagged from the weight of chisels and two long hammers. He unbuckled it and set it on the deck beside the entranceway then sat beside me. He reeked of sweat and fertilizer. His face was flushed with heat exhaustion. He emptied the first pitcher into his glass and chugged the ice-water. Streams dripped across his cheeks. His silver ponytail hung to the middle of his back. He finished, gasped, and filled his glass again from the second pitcher. He shoveled rice and picadillo onto his plate. His dark eyes followed our conversation as he chewed.

"The chief has us bolstering the partitions in the holds with shims and shoring timbers. It's hot and sticky as shit down there." Rafa rolled his eyes as he spoke. "We're running straight for a storm that's coming at us through the Yucatan Strait. Could be on us by late tonight or early tomorrow. Hope you're ready. That alley which joins the Gulf to the Caribbean is always rough." He shook his head.

The rest of the crew trickled in. One of the oilers came in with both hands bandaged. Rafa told us the young Panamanian had slipped in the engine room as we sailed out of the bay and into the Gulf. He'd singed both palms when he braced against the exhaust casing. Chino helped him fill his plate and set it down across from the Mexicans.

After lunch, the four of us finished strengthening the partitions in holds three and four. The Mexicans finished No. 5 and started No. 6. Lupe and Enrique carried the lumber. Coño limped along and did the hammering. The 6 x 4 timbers were as heavy as tree trunks. They took two to carry. Splinters pierced my gloves and the sleeves of my coveralls into to my skin. Each of us stopped every so often to pull off a glove, or roll up a sleeve, to pull out a sliver of pressure-treated pine. But the seas were calm without wind; the sky gray and cloudy. *Trader* ghosted along with heavily laden holds in a calm ocean—the "big puddle."

Tomas left us for the wheelhouse just before 1600. And we loafed the last two hours before chow. We sweltered in our grungy, sticky coveralls. Our knee-high mud boots kept most of the gritty dust out, but my feet sloshed in sweat-drenched socks. We were miserable. So with the timbers secured, Rafa let us sit the last hour.

Trader gently swayed. Rafa and the carpenter smoked a couple of cigarettes apiece. I leaned my head back on a timber and stretched my legs out on the coarse fertilizer. The hatch cover was only about four or five feet above me. I closed my irritated eyes. Scarlet sweat dripped from my forehead, nose, and neck. Heat radiated from the hatch cover overhead. I sank into the sandy texture beneath me as if I was in some strange desert-oven.

After chow, I went by the galley and shook Gordo's hand. He didn't say much. He fixed me a plate of leftovers: pork chops and plantains again. That was ok, I'd be hungry later. After a shower, I lay in my bunk to await midnight and the expected storm through the Yucatan Strait. The engines grumbled down the passageway. The guitar-man kept silent.

10:
YUCATAN STRAIT

At 2330, I ate leftover pork-chops and plantains, cold and greasy. *Trader* pitched and rolled. Gusts sprayed my porthole with salty mist. Rafa had said a storm was barrelling at us. I climbed into knee-torn blue jeans, pulled a windbreaker over a t-shirt, and tied on my paint-covered boots. The navy blue windbreaker had Miami International Boat Show written in bright red letters on the left and a bright yellow anchor sewn above. The chief had to know who I was. Maybe I could get him to talk about Roby's disappearance. He had to know Roby lived in Miami. Seeing Miami written on my jacket might spark a reaction. FDR had once said, "The truth is found when men are free to pursue it." What had happened to Roby? That was the truth I sought.

There was enough time to get some coffee. I went back to the mess through the dim heaving passageway and around the stack. Voices murmured down from the officer's mess. The steward left a full thermos for the helmsmen and the oilers every night after chow. The compartment was empty. The television was loud. A Mexican newsman ranted over the rolling beat of the diesels. I watched the fuzzy picture and poured two

Styrofoam cups full of the warm, black syrup, stuck a few sugar wrappers and cream-cups in a jacket pocket, and covered the coffee with a sheet of aluminum foil. No lids.

The bridge was three decks overhead. I teetered and balanced up the ladderway as *Trader* rolled. I leaned against the bulkhead, waited for her to come back, and moved up a few steps. The ladderway was on the starboard side of the stack and six 180° turns later I got to the chart room. On the chartplotter, a glowing line led from the northeast side of Galveston Bay bearing 130° southeast through the Gulf to the mouth of the Yucatan Strait. Just northwest off the shelves of Campeche Bank, a little Δ marked our last way-point: Latitude 26°—0′ North, Longitude 90°—0′ West. *Trader* was somewhere southeast of that point.

On voyages with the old man, my nights had been spent on the bridge, gazing at distant lights, determining if they were green or red. Or, in this tight chart room, leaning over the teak desk listening to his calculations and explanations then neatly placing a used paper chart in its giant drawer. And other times, catching Roby's finger between the parallel slide-ruler, or pricking him with the dividers.

Licenses and *Trader's* Lloyd's registry certificate hung in frames. A fire extinguisher hung from the bulkhead left of the black curtain that blocked the light to the wheelhouse. Another black curtain was pulled over the starboard porthole. A chronometer ticked above the chart desk. The clock read quarter to midnight. Many a shift, the old man had taught me navigation: dead reckoning, piloting, reading charts (magnetic north vs. true), or taking bearings from a pelorus mounted on a binnacle on each wing. The different ways of working out the Sailings—he was old-school, even though the ship had GPS now. But *Trader* was old-school, too. There weren't many left like her. But what she carried couldn't be stuffed into containers. He used to say, "In the days of the sail, computing longitude wasn't even possible. They just reached their latitude and then made 'eastings' or 'westings'—parallel sailing."

I'd always struggled with the math and geometry. I preferred to grip a wooden spoke of the helm, fight a rough manila hawser and learn knots, or even bang away at a rusty deck with a chipping hammer. Roby had always followed me. We'd chipped rust, brushed red-lead all day, and then fished with hand lines all night until our hands bled. All just to show the old man how tough we were. I'd climb a mast and Roby was right behind me. The old man had us cleaning out bilges when we were kids—good for morale. Hell, we'd learned to salute before I was eight; Roby was a little runt.

The ship slammed quivering into a trough. I moved forward and pushed aside the thick, black linen drape separating the lighted chart room from the dark bridge—dividing memories from my present purpose.

The bridge was black. I wavered, holding a cup in each hand, and waited until my pupils widened. I focused on the orange light that glowed from the face-mask hooded around the radar. The repeater stood bolted to the deck in front of a window. I spread my stance to shoulder width for balance. The cup holders were on the bulkhead by each wing exit. I stepped to the starboard wing and pushed the coffee cup into the holder directly in front of the chief. I turned and faced him, hoping he'd see the writing on my windbreaker. "Here's coffee, Chief." He sat in the captain's chair; a dark, silent profile with a neatly-tied ponytail sticking out from under a billed cap.

"You're early," he muttered. "Tomas, want some coffee? I have some brewing in the officer's mess." He spoke to Tomas in a surly whisper but his head didn't turn. Though I couldn't see his eyes, I knew he was inspecting me. Did he really have coffee brewing?

"No, gracias. It will keep me awake; I'm ready for sleep," Tomas said. I took a sip from mine—stale and thick. But I needed the caffeine. I chugged it down, tossed the cup into a basket, and bent my knees as the ship rolled.

Spray covered the fourteen large, thick windows that spanned the wheel house. A dim light glimmered high on the foremast. It pitched into the dark ocean. Then a wave crashed over the fo'c'sle and the light climbed into the sky. I steadied my stance and gripped the railing under the window. She rolled hard to port.

Trader pitched up, and I staggered to the helm. I braced on the steering console in front of Tomas and stood to his right. "Ready to relieve you," I said out loud so the chief could hear. Tomas stepped out from behind the wheel but kept hold of the top spoke. I slipped in front of him, grabbed the spoke he held just below his hand, stepped up on the platform, faced and took the big wheel.

"I have been relieved by Cesar, Chief. Steering 130 degrees." Tomas released the helm.

"I have the wheel. Steering 130 ° southeast, sir." I gripped the top wooden spoke with my right and quickly clasped the third one down with my left. I glanced at the dark figure on the starboard side. He crouched in the chair.

Tomas tapped my shoulder. Said, quietly, "He wants the gyro-pilot off because there's a storm coming from the starboard side blowing northeast. He's going to change course sometime before morning and point the bow south—straight at it. There're some shallow reefs north of the bank, and even more that border the pass through the strait."

"OK. Thanks, Tomas."

"Buena suerte. I'm going to bed." He patted my arm again and left. The wheel felt heavy and rebellious. I had to carry the rudder a point starboard to steer 130°. I rearranged my grip so I could push the top spoke right instead of pulling it. The large wheel had eight spokes. I kept upward pressure on the lower spoke in my left hand as if I was doing a half-curl with a ten pound dumb-bell. Enough curl to keep it from falling but not enough to actually lift it.

I glanced at the gyrocompass's lubber's line. The compass was mounted on top of the console and marked 129°. Inside the console, and visible through a little window from the top, another line indicated the rudder angle. I put the rudder one more spoke to the right. Zero meant the rudder was amidships. It could swing 35° to each side. Each spoke turned the rudder one-half degree. I locked my knees back to get comfortable on the wooden platform a few inches off the deck, and kept my eyes glued to the compass eighteen inches in front and under my chin. Then a wave crashed across the starboard bow. The ship yawed left to 126°. The wheel tight in my hands, I added another point of starboard rudder, waited and waited. After two or three minutes she started to swing back on course, so I took off rudder to meet her.

"How does she go?" The chief seized the right moment to check my heading.

"Bearing 128 degrees, coming to 130 now, sir."

"Wind's picking up. Might need to carry another point to the right. Keep her so." His voice was low and throaty.

"Yes, sir. Steady at 130° now sir." I was in for a workout.

"After sunrise, once we've sailed by these shoals, and turn toward the pass, you can let Iron Mike take over," he grunted, hoarse and slow.

"Yes, sir." He was testing me again. A twelve inch brass lever on the left side of the console engaged the autopilot. I stayed focused on the compass.

"With this wind and these seas against us we won't get through the strait until late tomorrow," he said.

I'd been aboard a week now. It was September, and still hurricane season. I wondered whether the approaching storm was a hurricane, or just a nasty thunderstorm. But facing any storm with a heavy bulk cargo could be ugly.

The chief got up and looked into the hood of the radar for several minutes. Then he grabbed the night vision binoculars and slid open the starboard door. He paused as the ship rolled and then stumbled over the coaming out onto the wing. The wind whistled. I struggled to keep the heading and rocked back on my heels with the ship's motion.

After five minutes, he stepped back in, grasped the railing under the front windows, and marched across the bridge. Leather boots squeaked as he passed in front of the helm and out through the portside doorway. Ten or fifteen minutes later, he came back in. The wind howled and hissed again until he slammed the sliding-door. As he swayed by me, he glanced directly at the left side of my jacket. The red letters glowed like little flames in the dark. He said nothing. He returned to the captain's chair with binoculars hanging from his neck, and perched there like a hawk waiting for prey to scurry from cover.

I lost track of time, absorbed with staying on course. I stood on the left side of the wheel, kept pressure on the top spoke with my right, tugged up with my left to carry two points starboard rudder and barely held 130°. The wind and seas blew *Trader* hard toward port. Yellow gear staggered along the main deck near No. 2 hold—probably Rafa checking the partitions. Waves smashed the starboard bow and beam. She rolled like a canoe in a raging river.

Around 0400, the second mate busted through the black curtain from the chart room. "Here to relieve you, chief," he said and barreled into the railing under the windows. He took hold and braced. She pitched up and rolled to port.

"No, wait until I point the bow into the pass and then I can tell what this storm's going to do. But bring me some coffee," he grumbled and swayed back strapped in the chair.

"Right away." The mate turned, waited for the next roll, and disappeared through the chart room again.

It was easy for me to stay balanced—I held the wheel. I was part of her. As if embraced in a dance, I leaned forward and up close against the wheel when she dipped into a trough. I tilted back with stretched arms and held the spokes when she pitched up; bent my left knee to shift my weight and swayed left with her as she rolled to port; bent my right knee and came back with her when she swung to starboard. My right hand was high on the top spoke—her neck and shoulder; my left hand held the third spoke low—her hip; side to side, back and forth like I was dancing a samba with a girl in my arms—a girl with green eyes. I'd missed that dance. I hummed the melody and thought of the lyrics to "Suavecito" by Malo:

"Suavecito, mi Linda—ay.
Suavecito.
I never met a girl like you in my life.

80

The way that you hold me in the night.
Suavecito.
Suavecito, mi Linda—ay."

For a little while, I forgot my troubles—forgot the scowl I veiled. I forgot the chief was on the bridge. It was just me, *Trader*-girl, the compass, and the sea. The waves were rough but not more than ten-to-twelve feet. The bad thing was that the wind and waves came broadside across the starboard beam, so she rolled hard to port and then swung back. But I didn't care. I had the helm. The chief might determine her heading, but moment by moment, I held her fate—everyone's fate. I hummed my song. And steady, steady and true, she went for me, against the pissed-off sea and bitching wind.

Then the mate stumbled through the curtain again. He balanced the chief's coffee. "Su café, chief," he murmured. He fought to keep his stance and waited for the Soldier to grasp the cup. The chief took it from his hands and gave him the full cup I'd brought.

"Dump that one over the side," he said and turned toward the helm. I hadn't met the second mate and it was difficult to see him in the dark wheelhouse. But he looked thin in his blue coveralls. His light, blondish hair fell over thick black-framed glasses. His bright-white tennis shoes squeaked with every step. He took the cup from the chief's grasp, staggered to the starboard door, slid it open, and marched out into the howling wind. A salty mist whooshed through the open doorway. He stumbled back over the coaming as *Trader* rolled, then he slid the door shut. It slammed, and rattled the glass.

He sauntered across to portside and raised his hand as he passed in front of me, then took a second set of binoculars out of the case which hung from the bulkhead, slid the portside door open, and wandered out onto that wing. Again the wind and spray rushed in. The door bashed and the glass clattered.

The chief got up from his chair, peered into the radar-mask a few moments then disappeared into the chart room. He returned and barked, "Right rudder 15 degrees, to 160°."

"Right rudder 15 degrees to 160 degrees—yes sir." I was steering 130°. The sea was turbulent, but I didn't want to swing too far. So, I turned the wheel even less, only ten degrees, and waited for her to swing. *Trader* pitched fore and aft as she approached 150°. I added two more spokes and as soon the compass read 153°. I put the rudder at zero to meet her swing.

"How does she go?"

After three or four seconds I sang out, "154 degrees, sir."

"Mind the rudder."

"157, 158, 161."

"Keep her so."

"Steady at 160 degrees now, sir."

"Very well." He moved closer to the console, glanced at the compass and then at me, and went out on the starboard wing. The wind charged in. The door crashed and rattled closed. The second mate opened and closed the portside door. He cussed and brushed back his wet hair with both hands. He pulled out his glasses from his top pocket, shook and brushed back his hair again, and wiped the lenses of the binoculars dry with the underside of his shirt. He stood clasped to the railing and eyed me. I concentrated on the compass. The chief came back and perched back in his dark corner.

We kept that course until El Indio appeared through the chart room at 0800. "Ready to take the wheel," he said.

I wasted no time. "Steering 160 degrees—I've been relieved." I let him cut in on the rolling and pitching dance with my girl. He was a thin-nosed, dark-skinned little guy not much more than five feet tall, but thick and wide shouldered like a stump. He wore the ship's blue coveralls and a dirty red-knit cap. He jumped up on the platform and repeated the course as I edged around him. He belonged there. The compass was just below his eye level and his stout arms rested at a comfortable right angle gripping a spoke with each thick brown hand.

Before I left the wheelhouse, I glanced out at the dark morning sky through the salt-bleached windows. An ominous dark mountain of clouds blocked the pass to the Yucatan Strait. A centurion sent from the Caribbean Sea to test our resolve—my resolve. The sea rolled white with foam in front of the black mass like frothed saliva spit out from Poseidon's rabid breath. I wondered whether it was smart to push on any farther, but my fate was in the hands of others. The chief watched me move toward the chart room. "Be back at 2400," he barked. I nodded and left.

Suddenly I had to piss. I bounced down the ladderway to the head and then to my bunk. I didn't want to eat.

In my cabin, I pulled the mattress off the bunk and stretched it on the deck. It was useless to sleep above. As I lay there rolling side to side, all I could think about was the silly little prayer children say, "Now I lay me down to sleep, I pray the Lord my soul to keep. If I should die before I wake, I pray the Lord my soul to take."

I didn't feel silly saying it, though.

11:
RULES OF THE ROAD

*T*rader pitched and rolled hard that night; I slipped off the mattress I'd stretched on the deck. My temple bumped the bulkhead; a sharp chunk of rust needled into a cheekbone. I slept dressed, with boots on. The ship thundered into a wave. I volleyed across the cabin. A barrage followed: a second and a third, as though I was on a mechanical bull. I landed legs wedged apart in a triangle against the corner; my ass bounced off the deck. My stomach fluttered, muscles tensed. I waited for a break, jumped up, and tumbled down to the crew's mess.

Dishes clattered. Sailors cussed. Only spoons or fingers—a fork could put out an eye. Forearms and elbows lassoed each plate. Chests pressed against the table; plates pushed into each chest. Half-filled glasses clutched between thighs. Raising food to the mouth became a timed motion. Everyone leaned forward, eyes fixed on his food, corralled with a bear-hug, like inmates in a prison cafeteria.

The deck gang had been split into three shifts. I spent the afternoon with the carpenter and Tomas checking partitions. We entered the holds with Mag-Lites and crawled over the red, gritty, sticky fertilizer. Then we leaned against and pushed on the boards and timbers to see if they would give, and nailed down anything that had shifted. We tightened or lashed down loose tarps over each hold to the cleats along the hatch stiffeners and searched for leaks. Tomas headed for the wheelhouse before 1600. The Mexicans worked from lunch to midnight. Rafa and one of the oilers scrutinized the holds from midnight through the morning.

Checking the cargo was a crucial and constant vigil. The sea's relentless pounding could loosen or snap a partition and cause the fertilizer to shift. Or, seawater could seep into a hold, drench and ruin the cargo, add weight, and disturb the balance. Either way, the ship could list, and the wrong wave could broach her over.

In the distance, the black thunder-dome of clouds still blocked the 120 mile-wide stretch through the Strait. The sky turned ever darker shades of purple as we approached the channel. No birds. No sunshine. Just squall lines: fast moving curtains of sharp slanted gray rain beneath dark cloud-bands. One after the other, they brought ten-to-fifteen foot breakers that smashed the bow like tanks protecting lines of soldiers. White water soared halfway up the forward masts. Spume engulfed the fo'c'sle and reached No. 1 and No. 2 hold. Brute waves splattered the decks. She dipped into each trough. The ocean swirled up to the gunwales. The stern rose high enough to expose half the screw. Every now and then, I tasted the pork chops I'd eaten for lunch.

Moving around on the main deck was a feat of stupidity, but it had to be done. Not doing it was negligent and foolish. Benjamin Franklin said, "A little neglect may breed great mischief."...so for want of comfort the ship might be lost.

85

My old man had once told me the story of his cousin from Asturias who had owned a shipping company in the south of Spain. The Spanish vessel's port-of-call was Valencia. She'd tried to cross the Mediterranean overloaded with wood stacked high on the deck. Rough seas had soaked the wood. It became so water-logged that the weight violated Archimedes' principle of displacement. In other words, the wood was no longer buoyant. During the wee hours, the radioman gave a last dispatch crossing the Straits of Gibraltar. Then she was swallowed by a massive wave and went straight to the bottom like an anchor let go from the capstan. All hands lost.

I climbed out of No. 6 at 1800, staggered on the main deck, and scaled the ladder to the shelter deck. Before I reached the top, the ship pitched up and plunged into a deep furrow. My wet boots slipped from the rung I stood on. Two rungs below, my knees banged and broke the fall. I hung, clenched to the handrail, regained my footing, and crept up the last few steps one at a time. Blood trickled down my shins.

I paused under the shelter of the aft castle and clutched the portside bulwarks. My knees throbbed. I looked out toward the passage. We were getting closer. I could just make out a red beacon far out in front and to port. That had to be the western-most point of Cuba—Cabo San Antonio. Off to starboard—Cabo Catoche, the northernmost point of the Yucatan. There was a lighthouse on Isla Contoy just thirty miles north of Cancun, but I couldn't see it yet; clouds clustered overhead.

My stomach wouldn't hold down food, so I showered and washed out the gashes in my knees. The fall had torn a quarter-size chunk from each knee-cap. I washed out the divots then went by the crew's mess and carried coffee back to my cabin. I waited for my turn to dance with *Trader*-girl again. And have a second stab at the chief.

At 2330, I put on my jacket and left. I trotted, slipped, and bounced up the ladderway, and careened into the chart room. The last way point was at latitude 23°—0′ North, longitude 86°—0′ West at 1930 hrs. Then I pushed through the black curtain into the wheelhouse. Tomas steered. The chief was in his dark chair—his ponytail profiled. I clutched the railing below the windows and looked across the ocean.

Hordes of tumbling whitecaps charged *Trader*. The legions of white-foamed goliaths crammed the pass like Spartans at Thermopylae. They gathered up in the dark, toppled their white peaks, and battered the bow. Spray soared high and over the decks. The glass vibrated and clattered. Stunned, I braced on the handrail for a second, then floundered to the wheel. "I'm ready to relieve you, Tomas." We bumbled around each other and fumbled with the spokes as I wobbled in behind the helm.

"I have been relieved, Chief. Bearing 165 degrees and carrying two points starboard rudder."

"I have the wheel. At 165 degrees with two points right—Chief." I quickly clamped each of my hands to a spoke.

Tomas tapped my shoulder. "Vaya con Dios," he said with a low, mournful frown. Even in the dark, his skin was gaunt; his dilated pupils betrayed his fear.

Trader wasn't making much headway. I guessed less than seven knots. She was now in the fairway; the red beacon was visible portside. The rule was Red Right Returning; we were headed out. On the right, off Contoy, a white light flashed. It repeated a group of three flickers and eclipses in fifteen-second sequences. The winds bottlenecked between the two points. The current and the waves pushed northeast. It seemed impassable.

Why not drop anchor leeward off Campeche Bank and let the hell-bitch storm pass? But onward *Trader* brawled and the chief bounced about strapped into his dark corner.

As I steered through the fairway and *Trader* plummeted into another depression, mast lights approached in line with our bow. When two vessels underway are in a head-on situation involving risk of collision, they are defined as meeting end on or nearly end on. Each has to steer to the right so as to pass on the port side. An essential nautical rule drilled into my head from many summers at sea with the old man. "Chief, ship ahead."

"Mind your wheel. I saw it already," he barked.

"Steering 165 degrees—sir," I snapped. At that instant, Captain McMorris burst through the black drape from the chart room. I froze. He wobbled to the radar and clenched the hood with both arms. He leaned his tubby gut against the unit and stared through the viewer. I watched him and waited for the inevitable.

The rule goes on to state that in a head on meeting neither vessel is privileged. Therefore, each vessel is burdened with the duty of avoiding a collision. McMorris finally raised his face. "She's still a mile off, but she has the wind and seas." He gazed through the salt drenched windows at the shifting lights. "Right five degrees to 170 and hold steady."

"Right rudder south by east to 170, captain." He recognized my voice, turned and after a quick glance reached for the binoculars. "Chief, give me a blast. And again at a half mile." He wobbled out on the port wing. The wind howled and swirled spray into the wheelhouse until the sliding door slammed.

The chief slid over to the horn handle, yanked a long, ear-numbing blast, and moved to the radar. I turned the wheel five degrees, but eased off the rudder quickly to avoid swinging too far. When I glanced at the compass, it read 172. I eased off a spoke and she rolled to 170°. I looked up and out through the port side windows and back at the compass; glass—compass; glass—compass. Then I saw the mast lights again as we plunged into a trough. A red lamp on her forecastle—a RO/RO vessel—huge. Not more than five hundred yards off. The chief pulled the horn again. I jumped. I was so engrossed with the mammoth, the deafening blast startled me. The beast roared back a blast and McMorris remained on the wing long after she passed by.

The wind ransacked the wheelhouse again when he returned. "Good steering, Cesar. She was a big one." He chuckled. I felt the chief's eyes. "Chief, do you know Captain Santino's oldest." My gut jumped. I turned toward the chief's black corner and nodded.

"Oh yes, we've met," he said. The son of bitch had known it all along.

"Well, this gale should pass by in an hour or two. So, I'm turning in. Buenas noche," Captain McMorris said with an American accent, and disappeared through the chart room.

Silence lingered the rest of my watch. Only real sounds could be heard: the rushing wind, the bashing sea, the creaking bulkheads, the clattering glass. I thought of a maxim by John Dryden: "Secret guilt by silence is betrayed." My thoughts raced through different scenarios. He's probably known it since the first day back at Port Everglades. Then Coño is his henchman; and he was trying to kill me. He has to know what happened to Roby. He's hiding something. I stewed, then remembered the compass. Holy shit. It read 175°. I was so pissed off I'd pushed too hard. Ten minutes later I had it at 171. I let it ease off with the current. Stay calm, stay calm. I thought of the "end on" rule again. Steer right; avoid collision. Steer to the right, I repeated to myself. And again, the helm drifted to 175 degrees. Again I eased off.

The chief never said another word. He sat in his perch, staring straight ahead and just did his job: checked the radar; checked the wings. *Trader* stayed heading 170° with my occasional lapses to the right or left. Soon the storm passed and the seas settled down.

When the little Guatemalan Indian appeared to relieve me, the harlot-wind had changed her ways and blew no more. The gale-storm conjured up from the Caribbean moved on to torment some other vessel or village. The treacherous gate of the Yucatan Strait was opened wide and the 7000 island-jewels exposed.

Just as I was exposed.

12:
CARIBBEAN SEA

We 'd battled the storm through the strait. Its sentry had finally called off the mauling wind and we passed south of the Tropic of Cancer into the Torrid Zone. Easterlies kept *Trader* in the doldrums. Her engines churned towards her southwest port of call; the danger waned.

Although the Antillean Sea was tranquil and the enduring beat of the diesels returned—no longer strained by the storm—I tossed in my sleep. I dreamt of fist-fights in dungeons, and drowning loved ones, and lurking sharks. I woke at 1100, sat up in my bunk, and planned my next move. The porthole let in the bright sunlight and a warm, salty air-stream. *Trader* swayed. I relaxed.

The chief remained a mystery. He knew Roby was my brother, yet had never said anything. My father was his superior, and the chief had never offered his condolences. I remembered something my old man always told me: "When you don't hold the best cards, play well those you do hold. Or, know when to quit." I wasn't quitting, so what cards did I hold? The same one I'd always held—I was Captain Santino's son. And, second, that I'd out fought the three Mexicans. I might not be a soldier, but I

91

wasn't a pushover. The chief knew these things. And he saw I wasn't leaving. He realized I wanted to know what had happened to my brother; that I knew he had been on the bridge that morning. There was only one thing to do—force the position. Push him. Ask him. What happened to Roby? You were on the bridge—right? Tonight, during my turn at the wheel, corner him. Ask for information.

After lunch I worked with Rafa, Tomas, and the carpenter on the main deck. The day was hot with a light breeze. Rafa and Tomas rechecked the bracing on all the partitions inside the holds. The carpenter and I stayed topside. Some of the booms had shifted in the storm. Two masts sustained damage to the yard-boom's lifting blocks: one high on the crosstree; another low to a heel block.

The carpenter cranked the winch and lowered the boom over No. 6. It squeaked and popped as it dropped the arm on top of the hatch cover. Then he turned the drum enough and slackened the greasy cable. I climbed the portside mast to the crosstree carrying a new block, a twelve-inch bolt with a nut and washer, and two 15/16 box wrenches. The bolt and wrenches I zippered into the pockets of my coveralls; the block I clutched in my right hand. I went up slow and placed both boots firmly on a rung before reaching for the next one. I strained to keep balanced and found the next rung with my left hand without looking up. I curled my right wrist around the rail while still holding the block, leaned my chest in, and pushed down with my chin on the rung in front. This entire voyage was a strain—a reach. The fragmented rust scuffed my skin. I cringed more each time. By the tenth rung my chin bled, but I didn't dare look down—couldn't turn back.

Twenty rungs later I ran out of ladder. I glanced at the deck wide-eyed, sucked in a quick breath, turned back, and focused on my grip. I clutched the rusted steel rungs with all my strength, gulped in more quick breaths then passed through the opening between the mast and the crosstree. The cool wind rushed by. I sat on the sun-warmed crosstree for a moment to steady my nerves. To fall from this height meant certain death. I breathed deep, grasped the railing, gritted my teeth, and climbed into the tiny crow's nest welded around the mast. On my stomach, I crawled toward the block, then wrapped a leg around one of the bars that supported the miniature railing. I wedged my left heel under the platform and stretched to reach the block. Blood rushed to my head. I locked my legs and clenched the thin rusty bar. The ship swayed. The carpenter looked up with one hand over his forehead to deflect the sun's glare. "Take your time, big balls," he yelled up. "Don't want to scrape you off the deck." I loosened the bolt one thread at a time, then tossed the chewed-up block to the ocean. It disappeared with barely a splash. I positioned the new one over and under the cable and bolted it to the angle-iron on the mast.

When I sat upright, my head throbbed. I leaned back against the top of the mast and dangled my legs over the narrow platform. I looked across at the bridge's windows. El Indio steered. The railing was sturdy; the breeze calmed my flushed face. *Trader* was in the Yucatan Basin now and probably close to the Cayman Islands. I wanted to be in the wheel-house, at the helm. To look at the chartplotter whenever I felt like it and know the exact position. I missed the leverage I was accustomed to with my old man as captain.

I squeezed the railing and gaped at the calm blue ocean striped with long, narrow islands of yellow kelp like wrinkled gold bars on a pressed navy-blue uniform. Cotton-white cumulus moved towards the western sun above the tangerine horizon. Flying fish scurried the surface. Seagulls zipped through and hovered aft. Debris floated by, snagged up in the weed-lines: shaved and splintered plywood, snapped boards, half submerged jugs, a rogue channel buoy, five bunched-up orange foam-buoys from a trap-line, several busted pallets, and many split branches. All causalities of the cyclone spawned in the waters of El Niño—what Peruvian fisherman had christened as "the Christ Child".

Miles of jagged weed lines, but not a vessel in sight. My back pressed against the top of the mast. I swayed with the gentle pitch and rested. I rehashed the sequence of events that had brought me out to sea and looked down at the deck. The whole undertaking seemed a precarious hunch—as precarious as my straddled position. The wind ripped across my face and tossed my hair.

The carpenter yelled up, "You OK?"

"Yeah, just getting my bearings." Blue water sparkled around the long brown and yellow weed-lines we paralleled, and the trash that didn't belong. From this summit, *Trader* looked small against the open ocean. With the slightest roll, it felt as though she could heave over. But she didn't. I glanced one last time, took a few deep breaths, and came down off the pinnacle.

On the deck, I removed the bent heel block from the starboard boom. The carpenter cranked up the winch and raised the portside boom. The winch squealed until the cable tightened and lifted the derrick off the hatch cover to a vertical position. I shackled the end of the cable to an eye-ring cleat on the bulwarks and the job was done. By the end of my shift, all booms stood ready for offloading cargo at La Guaira.

Gordo treated us to shrimp and rice for dinner. Coño and his brothers avoided me. I didn't even see them smoke after meals anymore. Afterward, I carried coffee and some bananas to my cabin and waited for 2400. Around 2100 Gordo strummed acoustic strings but he didn't sing. The Spanish melody filled the passageways.

Before I took the wheel again, I inspected the chartplotter. The last way-point marked latitude 19°— 0′ North, longitude 83°—0′ West at 1900 hours and bearing 133°southeast. At that time, *Trader* had been east of Misteriosa Bank and southwest of Grand Cayman. By now, she was over the Cayman Trench some of the deepest waters in the Caribbean. Far off to the west—Honduras; ahead—the Colombian Basin.

The chief slipped through the drape. "You read charts too, huh? Go take the wheel. I'll give you a new heading in a moment." He wore a short-sleeve khaki shirt unbuttoned over a white tank-top that was tucked into green army pants with a green-web belt. The belt had a brass buckle engraved with some military symbol. What was it? I couldn't see and I didn't want to ask.

"Sure do, sir." I stepped away from him, through the black cloth, changed places with Tomas, and took hold of the spokes. "I have the wheel. Bearing 133 degrees."

Tomas removed the toothpick he chewed and sang out the ritual words so the chief could hear in the chart room. He patted my shoulder and sighed. "Esta suave. With this nice weather, tomorrow afternoon—Venezuela. I have a girlfriend there; she has a sister." His breath smelled of mint; his drenched armpits, musty. He raised his eyebrows, wedged the toothpick back between two big front teeth, and left.

95

Trader churned at top speed now. The diesels hummed. Through the latched-open doors, the north-easterly blew a dewy mist across the wheelhouse. Over each wing, the skies were clear and filled with stars. The calm sea glistened under a gibbous moon; the running lights and decks gave off a phosphorescent glow.

The chief came out of the chart room and looked out toward the port wing. "Steer left and come to 107 degrees bearing east-southeast. That should take us through the Aruba Gap and close to Curaçao where we'll turn west toward La Guaira."

"Left rudder to 107 east-southeast." Steering was a cinch; the Yucatan had been the test. I put the wheel ten degrees port and waited for her to swing—no resistance. "120," I paused. "110, 108, 107—steady at 107 degrees now, sir." She dipped to 106°. I pushed one spoke to the right and she swung back on course. "Holding 107 degrees."

"Keep her so." He reached for the binoculars, slipped the strap over his head and went out on the port wing. Thirty minutes later he came back in. Shiny boots squeaked past the helm and out to starboard. Twenty minutes passed. He stepped back inside and peered into the radar for several minutes then settled into his chair—silent.

Through the front windows, bright moonlight showered the wheel-house. The platinum radiance glittered off the equipment. The brass rivets around the windows gave off a faint gold shine. The radar blazed orange around gaps in the hood as if a fire burned inside. Wind gusted across the opened doorways. *Trader* coasted in the soothing sea; waves sloshed against the hull. A welcomed contrast from last night's pounding and rattling; pitching and rolling.

I kept my head in line with the compass, but my gaze darted back and forth from the chief to the line that marked the course. I clenched a spoke and waited. The silence lingered on with an occasional splash from the wings.

He squirmed in his chair, hooked his heels on the frame, and leaned his right shoulder against the bulkhead. Then he took off the binoculars that hung around his neck and rattled them into the wire basket that hung from the bulkhead. His bronzed arms glistened in the soft light; his tank-top shone white.

I turned toward him. "Chief, you knew I was Captain Santino's son?"

He waited several seconds before answering. "What is it you want to know, Cesar?"

"What do I want? I want to know what happened to my brother—what else?" I shouted.

He cleared his throat. "I filled out a report—for the Coast Guard—and a second report—for the police. I'm sure your father told you."

"Yeah . . . yeah, he told me. He told me you were on the bridge."

"And?"

"And you didn't see or hear anything?"

"No, I did not!" He sprang down. His boots gave a loud thud. He yanked the binoculars out from the basket. The case clattered to the deck. He slid by me. "Mind your wheel," he snapped, and continued onto the port wing.

For an instant, I thought he was going to swing at me. I kept my eyes on him and forgot the compass for several seconds. When I looked back, I was still on course—107°. I kept glancing at him. He leaned against the bulwarks and crossed his arms on the railing. Then he cupped his hands and lit a cigarette.

The smoke trailed away. He took several long drags. His lips moved. He was talking to himself. He turned and looked at me while smoke escaped his moving lips then he stared up at the canvas of stars and puffed some more, and again looked my way. Finally, he flicked the butt, came back in, and stopped in front of me. "Cesar, tonight's your last night at the helm. I'll speak with Simon. He'll be ready to take back his watch tomorrow night."

"Hell, Chief, I'm just trying to find out what happened to Roby."

"I'm sorry that had to...that happened to your brother. I have family back in Peru; I wouldn't want anything to happen to them either. But Simon's better now. So sleep 'til lunch, then back with the deck gang."

"Back with Coño?"

"That's your problem." He put his hands over the compass and looked into my eyes. "Look, Cesar, I'm very sorry about your brother. I wish there was something I could have done. The biggest danger out here is from carelessness. Maybe he saw something in the water, leaned over the stern, and fell in." His voice was warm and caring.

"I guess so." The weight of his words drew me in. I let him persuade me. He took his hands away from the compass. With his left hand, he squeezed my right shoulder, then looked into my eyes. His face was dark and shadowed; his back was to the moonlight that came through the windows. He nodded and paused. His strong hand held my shoulder like a father's, waiting for me. For my acceptance. I hesitated, then nodded back. He stepped across the bridge, picked up the fallen basket, adjusted it into the clips, and climbed back into his chair. Back to where I couldn't see his face, only his profile. I thought of Frost's poem again. "It's treason to bow to reason."

The second mate relieved the chief at 0400. I stayed until El Indio relieved me at 0800. I skipped breakfast, slammed into my bunk, and punched the pillow until feathers came out one end. I covered my face from the morning light and slept until lunchtime.

13:
PUERTO LA GUAIRA, VENEZUELA

fter lunch I rejoined the deck gang. The chief assigned two of us to paint the bulwarks on the bridge wings. Slap on a fresh coat to spruce up and hide stains and cracks. McMorris paced the wheelhouse in bulged-out suede deck shoes, khaki shorts, Hawaiian shirt, and blue baseball-cap that read CAPTAIN on the front in white letters. El Indio was fixed to the helm; blue coveralls hung from his stumpy dark-skinned frame that contrasted with a thin pointy nose.

Tomas painted the port wing; I worked to starboard. I carried two five-gallon buckets. One was empty. The other two-thirds filled with white titanium dioxide. Its dense texture covered well, so I used a small sash brush for edges and corners, and a four inch flat brush for the bulwarks. First, I wiped the surface down with rags to take off some of the dirt and grunge. Then I painted over the rust stains, divots, and scaled, bubbled-up or cracked spots from the deck to the teak railing. I should've chipped out the failed paint but didn't. Thick long strokes from top to bottom; thin strokes close to the deck and underneath the railing up to the wheelhouse's sliding door. The blazing sun seared the deck but occasional gusts brought relief. The paint dried fast. Each hour, I boxed the soupy mixture between buckets to keep it from forming clumps. The sharp smell of oil pigments rose from the buckets. Back and forth, I shuffled about on the scorching deck; my thoughts drifted from my work to the chief's speech the night before. He'd appeared so genuine—so caring. It didn't fit him. But his words made sense. I brushed the thick white paint over the dingy bulwarks all day.

By late afternoon, I reached the railing. My right hand cramped up. The tang of solvents filled my nostrils and made me woozy. I stretched, and glanced down to the main deck. The back of green fatigues faced me. The chief stood with Coño beside No. 6 hold. The wind rushed by. They were two decks below. Too far to hear. But the chief's veins bulged on his neck as he spoke. He raised his forefinger in Coño's face. Coño kept both hands in the pockets of his coveralls, nodded, nodded again. The chief pointed at Coño's head, and with two fingers stabbed the middle of the forehead. Then he slapped Coño's shoulder shook his hand, and marched underneath my wing into the aft castle. Coño stared at the deck for a moment, hands mining his pockets, then turned and glanced up at the starboard wing; I ducked from sight.

Pork chops, rice, mashed potatoes, corn and beans, biscuits instead of bread, and extra helpings too—dinner was a feast. This meant we'd be working all night after mooring at La Guaira. During the meal, Lupe and Enrique jabbed and sparred, slapped and punched each other. The carpenter smiled for the first time. Tomas bragged about his puta-girlfriend who worked at the cantina. The oilers asked the steward if they could get haircuts after dinner. The TV played a Mexican western; a vaquero kissed his sweetheart. The crew exploded into howls and shrills, then a chant, "Cervezas, Cervezas, Niñas y Cervezas; Cervezas Cervezas, Niñas y Cervezas." A biscuit bounced off my head and hit Rafa in the face. He stopped eating, stood and braced the table, "Lupe—Cabron."

The chant ended when the chief walked in and stood between both tables, hands on hips and a scowl on his face. "All right, all right, that's enough," he shouted. The two kids giggled for a few seconds, then the mess quieted down. "Turn off the TV," the chief barked. Someone grabbed the remote and muted it. "The pilot will be coming alongside between 1900 and 2000 hours. It's the Hippo," he said. Everyone started laughing and jeering all over again. "Calm down, calm down, you shitheads," he said.

Tomas leaned over to me with his buck teeth sticking way out. "The pilot's fat as hell. He wears a harness, and we winch him up. Coño's brothers started calling him 'The Hippo', and it stuck."

I laughed. Tomas scratched his scalp through black curly locks. "I think he's from Peru or Colombia—the chief knows him. I heard that, some time ago, the fat bastard was in the army or something."

The chief held out both arms until everyone quieted down again. "Rafa, run the winch and boom on No. 6. I'll radio the pilot and guide him to the starboard side. El Indio is going to stay at the wheel 'til we dock. So—Tomas, take Cesar and stand by to help the pilot over the gunwales and unhook him from the cable." We nodded; he continued, "Coño, take your brothers aft and tidy up. And the carpenter can check on the fo'c'sle until we get the pilot aboard—clear?"

"Si—Señor—Chief," the crew answered. Lupe and Enrique kept joking, but Coño stayed serious. He was the only one who didn't laugh.

After dinner, we were back on deck. I went with Tomas starboard by the gangway. The wind gusted from the east and the sun fell behind the mountains that formed a backdrop for the port. La Guaira didn't have a natural harbor. Over a mile of breakwater-boulders formed a jetty to shelter the docks. Behind the breakwater, a paved wharf joined a roadway leading to the toe of the mountainside where the city's industrial yards and scrap yards had grown up.

Trader's engines were slow ahead now. I looked up at the starboard wing. The chief and Captain Morris were sprawled with elbows resting on the railing to the wing's coaming; binoculars pointed toward the mouth of the port. Waves bashed the jetty. White water splashed up in sequence as they marched down the row of boulders. Houses lit up the mountainside with yellow specks. Tomas and I kept our eyes on the mouth of the inlet in search of the pilot's launch.

"How long to offload, Tomas?"

"About two days for each set of holds," he muttered and mauled his green toothpick. "We'll do two at a time. One and four; two and five; three and six, and then. . . niñas y cervezas—niñas y cervezas." He chanted and smiled, the toothpick wedged between his teeth.

"So about six days… plus today?"

"Si—the port never closes but the cranes are slow. They truck the fertilizer straight to the factory to be processed, mixed, and bagged for sale." Rafa whistled through his fingers at us and started the winch. Tomas stepped to the bulwarks where the cable was fastened, loosened the pin, and released the small shackle from the eye-cleat. He kept hold of it. Then Rafa maneuvered the boom above us so the end extended a few feet over the side.

We huddled against the gunwales and waited. Dusk turned dark. The mountainside glimmered with hundreds of lights sprinkled across it. Below the highlands, the port's buildings and warehouses flickered, along with the masts of two or three other moored ships. Then I spotted the pilot's launch skipping out from the mouth of the port. The white fiberglass boat raced toward us spraying foam with every bounce of its bow. A blue light on top of its cabin flashed between the red and the green on each side. With every slam, a white splash filtered its lights into glittering prisms. Closer and closer the launch came skipping out of the gray fog.

Trader coasted up to the mouth of the harbor, running lights on. The diesels stopped rumbling and the launch thundered alongside the starboard beam, powered by twin 150 Evinrudes. The two-to-three-foot chop rolled the twenty-five foot craft into *Trader's* hull. The old tires hanging from the boat's port side squealed and with a puff of powdered rust the boat careened off *Trader's* side. The squishing and rubbing repeated several times before the pilot stood from the cushioned seats. He wore a white shirt tucked inside massive white pants. His gut hung over a black leather belt. The harness came around his large legs and around his plump arms and chest. It was more like a body-saddle. He clutched the top of the shelter cabin with his left hand and cupped the side of his mouth with his right. "OK, ready," he yelled, and staggered to the center of the launch as the choppy sea bounced it against our hull again.

"Go, Tomas," I said. Tomas gestured at Rafa and the boom whined, lifted higher and farther out. I tossed the cable down to the waterline. It beat the hull with a dull metallic thud before a sailor aboard the launch grabbed it and heaved in. Moments later, the Hippo was clipped to the cable. Shit, he was bigger than Gordo. The front of the harness had a large eye-ring centered on his chest. The sailor secured the pin and checked the shackle while the skipper kept the launch alongside. The Hippo grabbed the greasy cable with his gloves and Rafa cranked the winch.

Soon his white sneakers were well above the gunwales. He looked like a giant snowman in his white uniform. I thought he'd burst like a piñata from the pressure of the harness. He hung there a few seconds, then the boom came over the side and parallel to the ship, and the cable slowly dropped him to the deck. He took off his right glove. A gold watch glittered. He yanked at the leather crammed into his nuts and ass, scratched his armpits and glanced at me with a quizzical smirk. "I'm getting too old for this shit," he said, shaking his head. He was dark-skinned and his gray hair was oiled down with sweet-smelling mousse.

Pilot aboard, a blast came from the horn and I looked up at the wing. McMorris peered over the railing, his blue cap visible above the green lantern. He waved off the launch. It roared and parted a large wake of foam. The blue light above its cabin kept spinning as it led us to our berth. Tomas secured the cable to the cleat again and with the boom vertical, Rafa shut down the winch.

The pilot wobbled up the ladder to the shelter deck. He huffed and puffed with every step. His hips rubbed the rails each time he moved up a rung. The chief greeted him at the top with a sturdy handshake and pulled him up the last rung. Then he joked about something I couldn't hear, wrapped his arm around the Hippo's shoulder, and shook the giant beach-ball of a man. He helped him out of the harness and they disappeared into the aft castle. I turned and followed Tomas and Rafa to the fo'c'sle to prep for mooring.

The ship docked around 2100 and the hard work began. The night was clear with a cool breeze—no rain in the forecast. We removed all the tarps first. Then Rafa rolled back the hatch covers for No. 1 and No. 2. The smell of baked fertilizer punched the breath out of my lungs and burned my eyes. I covered my face with a rag, my eyes with goggles, and took shallow breaths.

We broke up into two teams, crawled down the man-holes with hammers and pry bars, shuffled through the gritty, sandy, reddish fertilizer, and tore down the partitions. After No. 1 and No. 2 were dismantled, we stacked the wood in the center of each hold and tied each bundle together with ratchet-straps. Rafa started the winch and lowered the boom. Tomas and I shackled two sets of hook and snotter to the hatch-whip cable, and Rafa hoisted the bundles out. We left each package of boards and timbers wrapped and strapped on the port-side deck beside each hold; the ship had moored on the starboard side.

We did the same with the remaining holds and then closed the hatches leaving No. 1 and No. 4 folded up and opened. At 0530, we left the holds in order and ready for off-loading at 0600.

I started up the ladder to the shelter deck worn out and craving a shower. I looked across the dark wharf. The mountainside glowed behind it with radiant homes; the night sky was packed with stars. In front of the warehouses, the pier had spotlights every hundred yards or so. Where *Trader* had moored, there were no other ships and the emptiness echoed the hammering that came from inside a warehouse. For several hundred yards, bollard after bollard stood without the embrace of a manila hawser. Fifty yards across from the ship, a guardhouse glowed with a dim yellow bulb. The figure inside leaned its head against the window.

The road outside the gate was the autopista—central highway. A dark streamlined car pulled up to the far gate. A Mercedes or a BMW. Someone got out, checked with the guard, and walked through the gate. He came toward *Trader*. As he came closer, I realized it was the chief. He was in gray slacks and black silk shirt instead of fatigues. He looked like a celebrity, not the chief mate of a cargo ship. He took long, hurried strides and swung his arms; his fancy shoes clicked on the concrete. Each step echoed across the empty wharf. I left before he reached our gangplank. Where the hell had he been? I remembered one of Murphy's Laws from a poster in my dorm: "If everything seems to be going well, it's because you don't know what the hell is going on."

14:
THE BLACK CAR

We crowded into the crew's mess at 0600. Gordo had a quick breakfast ready: piles of eggs, bacon, juice, and several large pots of coffee. From the pier, the roar of dump trucks thundered through the portholes. Trucks shot through the gates and positioned in rows beside the open hatches. Air brakes hissed each time one stopped alongside. A low, heavy beat of engines idling grew louder and louder. Sometimes, one beeped and beeped and then hissed

Enrique went to a port hole and looked out. "Cinco . . . siete y ocho." He held his plate just under his chin to shovel down eggs with a fork. The crew chomped and chomped watching him. Lupe jumped up and darted next to him. They huddled, shoulders touching, in dust-tainted blue coveralls, straight, thick, black hair shaved around the sides to their ears like teenage twins. Lupe moved to another porthole, stuck his head through, and looked toward the bow. Enrique kept counting. "Nueve . . . diez." Then Lupe hurried back to the table, sat down, and scooped more food onto his plate. I scarfed down two servings and a large coffee.

Stomach full, I loosened my coveralls and sipped on a refill. Where had the chief come from at almost four in the morning? And who had dropped him off at the gate in that ritzy car? Maybe he'd gotten laid? Yeah…maybe, but whose car was that?

After breakfast, Rafa started the winch for No. 1 and the carpenter operated No. 4. The drums turned and whined. The booms dropped. To each boom, we attached a grab-bucket with hook and swivel from under each winch's platform wherever they had ended up from the last trip.

A grab-bucket has two sides of equal weight. When it is dropped onto a dry bulk cargo, a guy-cable closes it and clutches the sandy cargo. The winch then pulls the full bucket up close to the top of the boom, the boom extends over the gunwales above the waiting dump truck, and a release-cable opens it and drops the load. It's slow, but simple.

The rest of the deck gang had tedious, nasty jobs. One man was stationed in front of a hold along starboard. Each man kept an eye on his bucket as it lifted out and trickled red streams across the deck. He signalled when the trucks were full and motioned the next into position. Inside each grimy hold, two more hands kept watch on the buckets and cables to keep them free of snags or crimps, to shovel out corners and sides, or to position the bucket if needed.

Tomas and I carried wide, square-point aluminum shovels into No. 1, and two spade-shovels for the corners. Inside, the heavy dust inflamed my throat and nostrils. The thick, powdery air burned my eyes. We wrapped rags around heads and mouths, and strapped goggles on.

Our rubber boots sank into the coarse russet granules, as if we were walking on Mars. We tucked the coveralls inside the boots to keep the gritty fertilizer from getting under the pants legs. I lifted my collar to my chin. I preferred to roast inside the thick cowhide than have one speck touch my sweaty skin. But the red crap still found uncovered places to fester into: around the rims of the goggles, gaps in the rags, into the boots, or through rips and pinholes in the coveralls. After a few hours, a rash broke out around my neck and between my legs. We scratched and cussed all morning.

The work pushed on. Each truck required between twelve and fifteen buckets, depending how well the bucket clasped the fertilizer and how heavily the truck was loaded. By lunchtime, the sun had us baked like battered meat wrapped in cellophane.

Just before 1130, Tomas and I plunged our shovels into a mound and scurried up the ladder to the main deck. A large brownish-red cloud hovered midship and the spillage from the buckets covered the starboard deck. During lunch, the wind swished away the cloud but the stench lingered. It attached itself to everything and everyone. I chucked up red sputum and blew out red phlegm.

On the pier, two lunch vans rolled past the guardhouse as we climbed the ladder to the shelter deck. The side of one read: El Pan de Cada Dia—Our Daily Bread. A high-pitched, ding-dong, melody resonated between the dusty ship and the dented, corrugated-aluminum warehouses. The truckers and stevedores rushed the wagons like a school of yellow-tail in a feeding frenzy. Next to *Trader*, two dump trucks idled half loaded. The music played on.

We washed up, ate, went back to work, and were covered in sticky filth again before the end of the first hour, bucket after bucket, truck after truck. The government here was running on fumes, but they still had money for fertilizer. Strange that the source of our toil and disgust would grow the crops that fed this country. That such an irritant could be so necessary, and in the end, even beneficial.

Dinner was delayed until after dark when the last truck left weighed down. When the work stopped, two holds were more than half empty. The food vans returned. The dock workers reeled around them again, and the church music accompanied the onslaught.

After dinner and a shower, I wanted to sleep but stayed awake and left my door latched open so I could hear down the passageways. The wind picked up. It whistled through my porthole. Across the narrow horse-shoe harbor, the sea crashed against the jetty. Foam and spray splashed up as high as a three story building and onto the far side of the pier. Fork-lifts dominoed containers in tiers. They shuffled the twenty-foot metal boxes from the railroad tracks to the pier.

From the officer's mess, garbled voices echoed through the dim passageway. I waited until the TV went off then tiptoed to the end, stood outside and listened. Empty. I crept halfway down the lit ladderway and stopped. The crew's mess was also quiet. I walked in and stepped into the shadows, away from the light that streamed in from the pier.

From the corner porthole, I had a clear view of the guardhouse. I leaned against the bulkhead and studied the shadows. Moths circled the spotlight in front of the warehouse. I thought back to the dead moths on Mom's front porch and wiped the cracked face of Roby's watch clean. Small screech-bats ambushed the moths that surrounded the white lamp. The moths circled the light and the bats darted through the moths. It looked like a game. But the bats were feeding and the moths were dying.

A soot-covered gray cat came slithering along the front of the warehouses. An overloaded dumpster stood canted against the fence. Trash littered the asphalt and rats plundered through the scraps. The cat paused at the corner beneath three payphones mounted to the siding. It spotted the rats and stood motionless, then rushed at them. The rats screeched and dashed through a hole into the warehouse leaving the cat to pick through the leftovers.

My eyes closed heavy and tired. The stink of the nitric dust reeked from the dock. The wind couldn't get rid of the odor; it kept me awake. Then two scrawny mutts came rambling down the fence-line, heads low, sniffing; their tails wagging. They pranced up to a garbage can behind the guardhouse. The bigger one stood on its hind legs and pressed down on the edge with both front paws. The can tumbled over and crashed. The lid rolled and clattered. The guard turned in his chair and stumbled out of the little shack with a Mag-Lite. He searched the ground, bent, gathered some rocks, and chucked stones until one squealed and both dogs scampered down the empty wharf, tails tucked, looking back.

It was after midnight. I'd be tired in the morning. My hunch had failed. Try again tomorrow night. I slipped back through the gloomy silent passageway to my bunk.

The next day we emptied No. 1 and No. 4, and switched the buckets over for No. 2 and No. 5. Later that night, I returned to the crew's mess and scrunched in the dark watching the gate once more. And again I saw only moths, bats, and desperate vermin.

On the third night, with No. 2 and No. 5 half empty, the sailors congregated in the mess room. They talked loudly and paced about. They elected Rafa as spokesman and he left for the captain's quarters. He returned twenty minutes later and announced, "Capitan has granted shore-leave until 2200." Cheering erupted and everyone raced to his cabin.

Some stayed on the pier and talked for hours on the payphones beneath the moth-swarmed spotlight. Coño and his brothers went shopping. I stayed in the crew's mess and watched the gate. Nothing strange happened. The shoppers all returned more or less on time and bounded up the gangway. At 2300, the second officer winched up the plank a few feet off the pier and left his post. I went to sleep.

By the end of the fifth day, we had No. 3 and No. 6 half empty. The next day we would finish. The weather had been favorable and we had made good time. I kept vigil again until midnight but didn't see the chief or the posh car.

On the morning of the sixth day, clouds packed the sky above the mountainside and the day was still and dark. The dry air turned cool and humid but it didn't rain till the sun hid behind the peaks. A light shower drizzled through dinner.

After dinner, the crew lined up outside the captain's quarters to receive their wages and be granted liberty. The following day, we would take on stores, bunker fuel, and head for dry-dock in Willemstad, Curaçao. Departure was scheduled for late afternoon, so the night was to be a drunken orgy at the crew's favorite whorehouse and cantina—*Las Señoritas.*

Trader had left Port Everglades on Sunday, August 28th and tonight was September 12th. I had worked fifteen days as an ordinary seaman for seven dollars an hour. Three days at the helm—though I doubted I'd get a rate increase. I stood with Tomas at the end of the pay line figuring what I'd earned. As a deckhand, from 0600 to 1800 minus thirty minutes for the first two meals; three days with eight hours at the wheel and four more hours on the deck should be a nice sum. So, twelve days with 11 hours and three days with 12 hours was 168 hours at seven bucks minus taxes—not too shabby.

The officers were paid separately so only sailors stood in line calculating. Some had paper and pencils. Some wrote on their hands. The aroma of Pierre Cardin, Brut, and Old Spice filled the passageway outside McMorris's quarters. Enrique and Lupe wore earrings and their hair was slicked with mousse. Coño had on a black Mexican sombrero with a yellow tassel laced through the rim, snake-skin boots, jeans, and a black silk shirt. Tomas stood in front of me in a white silk shirt and black slacks; a toothpick was lodged between his buck teeth.

After thirty minutes, it was my turn. McMorris sat at the head of the table where my old man had sat the day I boarded. He wore his captain's cap and a white t-shirt. His belly wedged up against the edge of the tabletop. The safe was open behind him. A cash box on his right; a ledger and stack of checks on his left. He handed me a ballpoint. I signed my check for $ 1,176, then he cashed the net portion of better than eight hundred dollars, and I signed the ledger that I'd been paid. A sailor, loose on a port in South America—it felt like a small fortune. I went back to my cabin and stuffed six hundred into a sock and crammed the sock into a work boot. Two hundred plus was more than enough to get smashed at a whorehouse.

The crew split into two groups. Rafa, the three helmsmen (El Indio, Simon and Tomas), the carpenter, and I left first. We clamored down the gangway to the pier and walked out past the guardhouse. I turned when we passed through the gate and saw Coño with his brothers and the Mexican oilers whom I'd never really met strutting down the gangway. Coño was last. The wind swirled across the dock and he adjusted his sombrero against it.

He dragged his right leg a little, so the Mexican gang slowed down and kept pace with him. Their cow-hide, snake-skin, and alligator boots clicked on the moist concrete like the heels of flamenco dancers on a saloon floor.

Outside the gate, the four-lane autopista was named Avenida Soublette. Tomas said the plaza and hotels were to the left on the road to Caracas, the capital. Tall buildings marked the horizon that followed the coastline. The streets were brighter in that direction. To the right was the seedy side of town. We turned right. Rafa and the carpenter led the way. Simon and the stocky little Guatemalan followed. The black leather coat he wore reached his knees. Tomas and I brought up the rear. We ambled along the sidewalk in front of the eight-foot chain-link fence that enclosed the docks. Paper, Coca-Cola cans, Corona and Dos Equis XX beer bottles cluttered the bottom of the chain-link. Fiats and VWs streaked by. Half a football field's length behind, the clack and tick of cowboy boots tracked our path.

The fence-line went a couple of miles down the brightly lit pavement. The docks were behind the fence; the highway lay on our left. The night was breezy and cool from the rain. The mountains darkened behind us in the distance, toward Caracas.

Past the end of the docks, the fence made a hard right and continued to the mouth of the harbor. Along the entrance channel, benches and palm trees dotted a parking lot. We crossed the autopista to the left and down an unpaved side-street. Potholes dotted the asphalt. I skipped over a puddle and swayed when I landed as if still crossing the Yucatan—my sea-legs hadn't stiffened yet. On the left corner was a small boat-yard, fenced and locked up. A black-faced, wolf-sized German shepherd barked at us as we marched down the street. It gnawed

on the metal fence until we passed the yard. On the right, a bait
and tackle shop was still open. The owner sat outside on a stool
with a beer in his hands. A whiff of fish rose from his stained
apron. He smiled; we continued down the cul-de-sac.

At the end of the dead-end, a neon sign read *Las Señoritas.*
Music throbbed out into the street. Hell, it was rock-and-roll.
Bruce Springsteen's "Glory Days" thundered from a jukebox.

They'll pass you by—glory days.
Like the wink of a young girl's eye—glory days.

I thought of college and the little blonde with the green
eyes.

"So here we are," Tomas said. The street was empty and
dark with only ten or eleven cars and a few Toyota trucks. The
front porch-entrance had several empty wrought-iron tables.
Rafa and the carpenter went straight to the bar and we followed.

On the stage, a cute little mulata danced topless in a g-
string. She had curly black hair, little titties with glitter around
her nipples, a slender build, and a pair of cantaloupes for a butt.
The smoky cantina was dimly lit and all the light fell on her. Five
dock workers sat watching. One smoked a cigar and all drank
Dos Equis XX. It was a week-day and they were the only men in
the dive, so we took over the center of the bar in front of the
stage. After only minutes, more girls came out of the back. One
ran toward us. "Tomas, Tomas, mi amor." She hugged and
kissed him. Then she looked over his shoulder and asked if we
wanted drinks, but the bartender, a dark haired, lanky, middle-
aged guy with a pencil mustache wasted no time in giving all of
us a Dos Equis. I didn't argue. It was ice-cold.

Tomas got up from the bar and started for a table. He turned to me with his arm around his girl's neck and pointed at the one dancing. "That's her sister. Name's Mia. Bring her to our table when she's finished."

"Sure."

"Oh . . . Cesar, this is Tañía."

I shook her hand. Tañía had long red painted nails and wore a white button-down blouse tied above her navel; tight shorts were stretched around her chunky thighs. She was braless; her nipples pressed against the cotton. She leaned her plump face into me and kissed my cheek with glossy red lips. Tomas yanked her back and they walked off to a corner table, embracing.

I turned to watch Mia dance. The next song was Santana's "Black Magic Woman." I hadn't expected American music—but then again, why not? Rafa ordered a round of shots—tequila. I slammed one down and bit the lime. Then, another round of beers. My head rushed. My gut burned. Mia came off stage and perched next to me. Soon Coño and the Mexicans walked in and grabbed a table. And more girls kept showing up. It was as if the place opened at midnight. I went to Tomas's table and Mia parked her muscle-bound butt on my lap. And then more tequila, and more beer. Then Rafa, El Indio, Simon, and the carpenter joined us, each pawing a girl. We pulled three tables together.

The Mexican gang established themselves at the tables across from us. Two girls stood next to Coño. One had her tongue in his ear; the other grabbed his crotch. He put his hat on the one that grabbed him and pinched her tits. A third girl brought beer and tequila for the Mexicans. Tañía and Mia got up and went to get more drinks for us. Someone turned the music up louder.

117

"So Tomas, how long you been on the *Trader?*"

"What?"

"How long you've been aboard?" I shouted over the noise.

"Oh...about two years."

"You know Roby was my half brother, right?"

"What...Captain Santino's kid? No...I...I didn't know that," he said, dazed and wide-eyed. "You don't look like him, or like Santino."

"No, I look more like my mother. She died and he remarried," I shouted over the racket. "He married my mom's cousin. And hell, I was so young—she's been the only mother I remember anyways."

The girls returned with a tray full of beers. Tañía sat on Tomas's lap and kissed him. Mia did the same to me. She had little breasts and I liked running my fingers through her curly black hair. She still wore only a g-string with a white t-shirt. Her exposed silky ass felt warm on my leg and smooth to my hand. I leaned close to Tomas's ear. "The chief was on the bridge that morning. He says he saw nothing."

"I didn't see or hear anything either."

"You were at the helm?"

"Yeah...but I never left the wheelhouse 'til we docked."

Tañía turned his mouth toward hers and kissed him. "Papi, it's almost two. I can get off at two and we can go to my house." Calling him 'Papi' – 'Daddy' – was a typical way for a girl to flirt with a guy she wanted. Tomas nodded and kissed her again.

"How 'bout the chief? Did he leave?" Tomas hesitated and kissed Tañía. "Well...did he?"

"Yeah, he usually walks the deck when we're anchored offshore waiting for a berth. He was gone for an hour."

"He didn't tell me that," I said. Tomas turned away and told Tañía to get her things.

She jumped up and skipped over to the bartender, spoke to him for a moment, and hurried back to our table. "Ready, Papi?"she said to Tomas. Mia looked up at me and asked if I wanted to go. I started to answer but noticed a black ponytail profile in a tight khaki shirt taking a seat with the Mexicans. He turned the chair around, straddled the seat, folded his arms onto the backrest. Then he faced Coño, and began talking with him.

"No, Chiquita.... not yet," I said, and handed her twenty dollars. "Go get some more beer." The girls' eyes followed our American money. Tomas and Tañía snuck out as I watched the chief. The bastard had lied to me. He'd said he'd stayed in the wheelhouse—didn't say he walked the deck. That pissed me off. I thought of Roby and began mumbling to myself, and feeling righteous and bullet-proof, saturated with the alcohol.

About the time the chief finished his first beer, a waitress bent to whisper something in his ear. He got up and went to the bar. The bartender handed him the telephone. He couldn't have said more than a sentence or two before he gave the phone back. Then he marched straight out to the street.

I scrambled to my feet and stumbled into a chair. It teetered back but I caught it, and staggered to the exit just in time to see the chief climb into the sleek black Mercedes I'd seen at the gate the first night in port. It purred down the alley toward the autopista with its dark tinted windows rolled up. The tag read *000*.

When I staggered into the bathroom, two dock workers stood in front of the mirror scooping white powder into their noses from a plastic bag one held. They watched me with menacing eyes as I pissed into the rancid, scum-covered urinal. I turned away; they wiped their noses and left.

Cocaine...Mercedes...cargo ship...Fort Lauderdale and Miami....a Chief Mate...weed-smoking Mexican henchman. I stood there pissing, spinning the facts like a tossed salad. That has to be it. That's what's going on. Hell, he's even friends with the Venezuelan pilot—that Hippo guy. The chief runs the ship—nobody would dare stand against El Soldado. With Coño and his brothers to help. Well...suppose I'm right, I still need proof. And hell what am I going to do about it—rat him out to McMorris? How does he get it on board? The Mercedes is the key. Maybe he went to load the shit up right now . . . .Or, he's setting it up for late tonight? The guard at the gate probably gets paid to look away.

I kept on with my buzzed brainstorming and returned to the table. Mia waited with a coy smile. "Papi, let's go to my sister's. The owner said I could leave at three-thirty."

"When does this place close?"

"Well...if there're plenty of caballeros—not 'til daybreak."

"A couple more beers first," I said. She pouted and looked around as if she wanted to leave, so I tipped her another twenty. "Soon...we'll go—soon," I said. She snuggled up to me and tucked the cash in the pocket of her t-shirt. I had my mind on the chief, but I didn't want to lose sexy little Mia. Besides, I couldn't sit there alone. She kept rubbing my cock and kissing my neck. And I was tempted. But family came first—that's right—blood first. I remembered a quote by Duc de La Rochefoucauld, "Philosophy triumphs easily over past evils and future evils, but present evils triumph over it." Well, this little sex-goddess wasn't turning me away from my path—my duty.

I kept glancing at my watch—Roby's Seiko—mumbling to myself and wondering if the chief would return. The tequila and the beer fuelled my guesswork. Why else would he have lied? All this had something to do with my brother's disappearance. It was naive to think otherwise. What had Tomas said when I asked if the chief knew the Mexicans smoked weed? What were his words? "He's worse"...or..."he does worse." And it couldn't be weed they were bringing into Port Everglades. It was too bulky—too smelly. No. Hell, I read about stuff like this all the time in Miami.

I couldn't contain myself—couldn't sit still. I gritted my teeth. Mia kept grabbing my crotch and rubbing her sweet little tush against my hard. I kept twisting and spinning the alcohol-laden scenarios around in my head as she licked my ear.

"Papi, it's four now. Come on. Let's go to my sister's."

I kissed her moist brown lips and gave her another twenty. "Go get me another beer and keep the change."

She kissed me and skipped to the bar, appeased and obedient. I glanced around the room and back to the entrance. Coño got up with a girl and went toward the back. In a dark corner, a flight of stairs led upward. They took them up. I glanced back at the entrance—nothing. Rafa moved to a dark corner and so did the carpenter. They started getting lap dances to a Latin beat. A fat girl danced naked on the stage. The drunks at the bar rolled bills into crumpled balls and tried to hit her shaved crotch. Laughs and jeers howled when someone scored. The floozy smiled and scrambled for her earnings.

I turned again to the entrance as the chief strode in. He went straight to the bar. After a minute, the bartender handed him a shot of something. The chief chugged it back and chased it with a beer. Then he joined the Mexicans, still at the table across from me. I squirmed as I watched him. He didn't look my way, but he knew I was there.

After a few swallows of his beer, Lupe and Enrique started jabbing him in the shoulder. I strained to hear what they asked of him but couldn't. He handed Lupe something under the table and the two teenage gangsters ran off to the bathroom.

Mia returned with my beer and parked her butt on my lap. I chugged half the beer down for courage, lifted her off me, and put her in the chair beside me. I'd seen enough.

I marched over and stood in front of the chief, leaned on his table, and stared down at him. "I know what you're up to. I figured you out." I slouched on my arms and swayed as I spoke.

"Shut up, fool. You're drunk." He combed back his thick black hair and tightened the band around his ponytail.

"Did Roby figure you out too? Did he?" I shouted over the music. One of the oilers clasped my arm.

The chief glared at me with cold eyes. "Fuck you, Cesar! Sit down!"

"I know I'm right. I saw that Mercedes—your connection. You think I'm stupid. I'm Cuban. I grew up in Miami. I know what's what."

"You nosy little punk. Just like your preppy little brother!" The chief exploded from his chair. I flinched back but he bashed the right side of my chin with the bottle in his left hand. Lights flashed. I coughed up blood and spat out tooth parts. Another ambush. I moaned and slithered onto a table, then plopped to the floor. A roar of garbled shouts and high-pitched screams encircled me and the music screeched on. I tried to scramble up on my hands and crawl away under a table but a boot cut off my escape and battered my ribs again and again. A second blow hammered my head, a third and fourth my jaw. The assault went on and I sank into a black abyss.

15:
DRYDOCK IN CURAÇAO

When I opened my eyes again I was stretched out on the back seat of a fast-moving car. It swerved and screeched. Someone held me down. My right eye was covered by a towel pressed against the side of my face. I guess, to soak up the blood pouring from my chin and mouth. Deep voices murmured around me. I flinched and closed my eyes again.

Soon after, I roused lying on an elevated bed. I gurgled, choked, and coughed up on an apron. I tugged on someone's white sleeve jacket. Strong arms held my wrists and my legs; my jaw twitched with needling pain; my head throbbed. Then black again.

Later I stirred and jerked awake. I squinted at brilliant sunlight through puffed up eyelids. Vision blurred, I still recognized *Trader*'s faded red and blue hull. The sun warmed my thumping head and swollen face. Arms carried my aching body up the tilted gangway and into my soft bunk. Then I dropped into a long dark dream.

"Cesar, wake up. Cesar, come on, wake up." A familiar voice. I raised my arm to rub bloated eyes and winced from the pain pulsating from my ribs. Gently, I wiped off the caked blood and gooey discharge. My swollen face tingled as if needles were being shoved into my skin. Gordo squatted sweating on a stool beside my bunk. McMorris stood next to him. The captain's red tubby face hovered over me, eyebrows furled. Tomas stood by the door with folded arms. I started to speak but couldn't open my mouth from the throbbing sting in my gums and inflamed jaw.

"Cabron estas vivo." Gordo's gold teeth glistened beneath his thick black mustache.

McMorris jumped in. "Cesar, glad to see your eyes open. A concussion can be dangerous. I assumed you wouldn't be able to talk, so here's a pen and notepad." He placed them on my stomach. "I need to know why this happened. The chief returned that night, cleaned out his cabin, and jumped ship in La Guaira. Coño, Lupe, and Enrique did the same. Now I've got three sailors and one officer a.w.o.l. and you have serious injuries. Not to mention that I have a hospital bill from La Guaira's emergency ward for almost 10,000 bolivares and you're still going to need an orthodontist to get fitted for partials here in Curaçao—you're missing five teeth and may yet lose more. Now, I need answers, sailor! I demand a report on my desk! Understood?" He glared. I gave a feeble nod. "The steward will check on you in an hour. Send it up with him." He stormed out.

Gordo shook his head. "You're lucky the chief didn't kill you. Well...I have a pot of chicken soup hot in the galley. I'll bring some. With a straw." He got up and wobbled his massive body around Tomas and into the passageway.

Somber and silent, Tomas studied my face from the stool beside the bunk. "Want me to bring you a mirror?" His voice quivered. I nodded. He stepped across the cabin to the sink and unclipped the mirror mounted to the bulkhead.

I cringed. My head was shaved and there were two large, puffed up, open cuts over my right temple. The right side of my face was black and so gorged with blood that I looked like a rotting carcass. A five-inch gash on my chin had over fifty stitches encrusted in dried blood, and my eyes were blue and swollen. Smaller slashes covered cheeks, forehead, and eyelids. I tried to open my mouth for a glimpse inside, gave up, and waved at him to take it away. I was marred—but still alive. The bastard. I groped for inspiration and got Nietzsche: "All that doesn't kill you makes you stronger."

Gordo returned with chicken broth in a huge plastic tumbler. A fat straw protruded. The scent of greasy chicken soup made me so hungry I sat up, leaned forward, and scooted back against the headboard that pressed against the bulkhead. Tomas adjusted the pillow behind me. I slowly grasped the big, warm glass and carefully seized the straw with the left corner of my mouth. It took several painful tries to suck up the warm, salty broth. The bitter sting electrified my gums and jaw with prickling pain. I put it down, indicated 'no' with my index finger, slid down from the headboard, and wedged my head back into the pillow.

"You know we're in Curaçao—right?" I nodded. "Well, you've been asleep for almost twenty-four hours without food. Try to eat," Gordo said. I glanced out the porthole at the faint lights against the dark sky. I was hungry and queasy but the salt was too much to bear. I closed my eyes and waited for them to leave. Tomas shuffled out but Gordo stopped at the doorway. "Don't forget the captain's report," he said, then ducked his head, stepped out, and latched the door open.

Gordo's reminder echoed. I thought of McMorris's precise question: 'I need to know why this happened.' Why? Because I'd uncovered the operation. In a burst of righteous stupidity, I'd flushed El Soldado out. In my clumsy, drunken rage, I'd discovered the truth I sought. Yes, he was smuggling coke on board. And...because of Roby, he'd attacked me. The bastard had killed Roby. Or someone else had . . . maybe Coño? Roby had probably seen something while fishing in the shipping lanes outside Port Everglades that morning. What should I do? I couldn't tell McMorris all this. There was no proof; just my speculations. I wasn't writing this down. Hell no! Dad would be questioned, and maybe implicated in the smuggling. What could I do? Tell the police? Where? Back in Port Everglades? In La Guaira? Here in Curaçao? The chief was probably in Peru by now and Coño and his brothers on the road to Mexico. They'd get away.

Roby's body had never turned up, so the Ft. Lauderdale cops had nothing. No body, no culprit, not even any drugs. In La Guaira, there was no evidence of a crime, just jumping ship, and that was for the port authorities and the Venezuelan immigration, if there was such a thing. And the Curaçao authorities had nothing to do with any of this.

I didn't know what to do, but I wasn't telling McMorris shit. I lay there weak and dizzy staring out the porthole at the distant light, notepad and pen still on my stomach. When I rubbed my face against the pillow case to wipe the drool, pain spiked through my jaw. The hour passed and I never wrote a word.

Knuckles tapped twice on my door and Chino entered in his white mess-room frock and black jeans. He carried an ice pack. I touched it to my swollen jaw, shuddered and hissed, but forced the pouch against a tender spot for almost a minute before needing a break.

"Keep trying," he said. "It will reduce the swelling. Where's the report?" I shook my head and showed him the blank notepad.

"I have to tell El Capitan," he said. I shrugged and he left, white high-top Converses squeaking when he spun on the deck. His steps faded down the passageway.

Not long after, the squeaky steps returned, accompanied by heavier fast-paced strides. McMorris busted in. Chino stayed by the doorway. "Cesar, what's wrong? I asked for your account of this incident."

He watched my shaky hand jot on the pad. *Not sure what happened. Drunk. I'll think some more about it.*

"Bullshit! I have to provide a report to Gulfstream Shipping and another to the Venezuelan port authorities. And I've got to tell your dad, too. I'm in the dark here. The crew members that stopped the fight and hauled you to emergency say they don't know. I need something to go on."

I shrugged.

"Write something down. I'll give you more time to think about it." He stood there several moments, scanned my swollen face, and gazed into my battered eyes. His chubby face was red and serious; his arms were crossed. Then he scratched his shiny head, sighed, and left.

I drifted back to sleep.

When the steward came in to check on me the next morning, I had a fever. He said my puffy lips were crimson-red and my eyes blood-shot. "You have a serious infection," he said, and dashed out. His shoes squeaked through the passageway and up toward the captain's deck. Soon after, McMorris returned. He looked me over, then assured me he'd have a nurse or a doctor come aboard.

Three tomblike hours twirled by with me wrapped in the sheet and quilt like my death-bed cocoon. Finally a dark-black nurse appeared at my bedside in a gleaming white uniform. She was from the dockworkers' and seamen's clinic at the Curaçao Dry-Dock Company. She spoke a melodic island dialect— Papiamentu—that sounded like a blend of African and Dutch. She understood English and Spanish, though. She was slender with strong arms. Her hair was in dread-locks, and she smiled a lot. My face burned and ached, so she wiped it with a damp rag, stung my shoulder with a tetanus shot, then put me on antibiotics: Keflex, 500 mg. four times a day.

During this feverish interlude, *Trader* entered a graving dock. I wobbled to my porthole and watched the maneuver. Inside the long, narrow, box-shaped basin, divers positioned a keel block and a bilge block in line with the docking plan. The vessel floated in and positioned above the massive supports. Pumps drained the water until she came to rest on the heavy-duty blocks. Hoists held her level to keep her from listing. Emptied of standing water, the sand-blasting of barnacles, spores, rust and old paint that coated the hull began. The loud shrill of high pressure air blasting grit against the hull echoed in the gated basin. The sand exploded on impact, creating a silica cloud that rose from the keel. I pulled my porthole closed and tightened the screw to seal out the thick dust.

Another twenty-four hours of drinking apple juice, sweating, and stumbling to the head at the end of the passageway went by before my fever broke and the swelling went down. Five times that day I wobbled to the end of the narrow tunnel, wrapped in a sheet like a dying ghoul, then back to my haven cavern. Outside, the blasting continued. Tomas told me the wet-blasting had begun inside the holds. *Trader* was getting a full makeover and so was I.

As my body recovered, my hopes decayed. I rarely left my bunk or changed clothes. I overslept and started locking my cabin door. Sometimes, I didn't even answer, especially if it was Tomas's trademark double tap. How truthful had he been with me? How much did he know? He had to know about the chief's contraband enterprise. That's what he'd meant by "the chief does worse". And how much did he really know about Roby's disappearance?

After five days in dry-dock, my temperature dropped and the swelling diminished enough for me to mutter syllables. My face remained badly bruised and I chewed only on the left. As McMorris had stated, five of my teeth had been booted out, all on the right side: three on the top and two on the bottom. I stayed in my cabin and refused to work on deck.

On the morning of the sixth day, I had an appointment with a dentist, who sent me to an orthodontist. The specialist x-rayed and molded jaw impressions and sent them to the adjacent lab. I returned late that evening with an uncomfortable set of partials that cut into my gums. On the way back to the shipyard, I sat up in the back seat of a black and yellow taxi, grinning into the rear-view and studying the bright white enamel and the metal clasps that kept my new teeth in place. Screw it, what could I do but push on. I forced a painful and cynical smile and paid the cabby, who left smirking and honking the horn. Then I marched to *Trader*, which towered on her supports. Beneath her, sand-blasting continued in shifts around the clock. I limped across the elevated gangway through the haze of sand-dust and locked myself in my cabin.

By dark on the seventh day, the workers had finished stripping the hull of all the barnacles and old paint. The dockworkers rolled scaffolds in through the thick slurry of grit-waste covering the dock-bed beneath *Trader*'s hull and locked the brakes on the steel wheels. Then they started spraying the stripped metal with the first coat of a zinc-based anti-corrosive. The odor pierced my closed porthole and reeked in the passageways.

Inside the holds, *Trader's* crew completed the pressure washing. Rafa, the three helmsmen, and the carpenter brushed the bare steel in No. 6 with red-lead until 1800. After dinner Tomas stopped by to visit.

I ignored the first few knocks but he persisted so I opened the door. "What's on your mind, Tomas?"

"Just to see how you are." His head was bowed. His shoulders drooped as if walking up the aisle to receive communion. I studied his posture. What did he want from me? I let him in. I'd pick at him and watch. The mouth lies but the body betrays. "You look much better, new teeth and all," he said and plopped onto the little three-legged stool.

I perched on the edge of my bunk. "Yeah—thanks. That's what you came to tell me?"

"Well…yeah…and…." He dropped his head and drew a breath through clenched buck teeth. "I was wondering. Did you write that report for the captain yet?"

"Why? What are you worried about?"

"Nothing." He stared at his dirty boots. "I just wondered why the chief did this to you."

Guile was not his forte. He had a conscience, so I pushed. "You know what, Tomas? I think you know exactly why the chief did this to me."

"What? No...I... I don't know."

"OK, want to play that game? I'll write what I think in the report."

"You can't suspect me of anything. I never leave the wheelhouse."

"Suspect you of what? You mean like helping the chief smuggle coke into the States?"

Tomas stared into my eyes. He brushed back sweaty black hair and wiped his lips. "El Soldado's dangerous, Cesar. He's ruthless because he's desperate. I'll tell you what I know if you keep me out of the report. And you can't repeat this. He knows I live in Maracaibo."

"OK, tell me and I'll think about the report."

"You give me your word, Cesar?"

"Yes—you have my word, Tomas." I squeezed his trembling hand.

"The chief is connected to the Colombians, I know this from Coño. The way he tells it, the chief's father once owned a tugboat business in Peru. The chief grew up working on tugboats. But when he got married he joined the military."

"So he's married? What's his real name?"

"Larosa . . . and he has a little girl, too. Anyways, years, ago, the Peruvian government organized a task force to destroy coca fields in the Andes owned by the Colombians. El Soldado was a sergeant in the task force. The Colombians caught him. But instead of killing him, they threatened him and his family, unless he crossed over. So he joined the merchant marine to move the stuff into the States for them. He climbed to chief mate, and now he's grown to be a powerful and feared operator. He's no one to mess with. Believe me."

"The black Mercedes—right?"

132

"I've seen it, too. But you can't tell McMorris. You gave me your word."

"I'll keep it, Tomas. Don't worry. I boarded *Trader* to find out what happened to my brother. The rest's none of my affair."

"Well, I never left the wheelhouse. That's the truth. I had nothing to do with your brother going overboard. And I feel terrible it happened—believe me. The chief always put a few hundred dollars in my pocket to be the helmsman when the launch would come alongside for a pickup."

"What do you mean, a pickup?"

"That's how he avoids customs in Port Everglades, even in Houston. A powerboat comes alongside the night before. Duffle bags lowered over the stern. It's quick…real quick."

"Roby must have seen it. When he went back to fish."

"He had to, and tried to tell your father. And the chief probably threw him overboard. Your father never suspected him. He trusted him . . . he was ex-military, and a chief mate, and all. And…I swear. I had nothing to do with Roby. And what could I do. He would kill me, too… and my family, in Maracaibo. He makes a phone call, and that's it. There's no mercy from these people."

I leaned back into my pillow. I played the scene over in my head. Each time it ended with Roby sinking to the bottom. People are cannibals. They feed on each other like the bats feed on the moths blinded by the light. I remembered a saying my grandfather told me before he died. "Life is like a henhouse; those on top shit on those below." He'd spent most of his life in Machado's military, and witnessed the atrocities Batista's ruling class had inflicted when he took over.

Tomas picked at black grunge beneath his thumbnail. "Well, I've said too much. Now you know what I know. Please Cesar, say nothing. I fear that man." He scampered out and closed the door behind him.

I got up and locked it after him.

16:
PORTUGUESE LEAVE

The next morning, I took a long hot shower, shaved around the sutures, pulled a few stitches out from the corners where the gash had begun to mend and gently washed my purple-red face. I popped out the partials and filled the divots and abrasions with peroxide. The right side of my cheek sagged and my lips drooped. I looked older. Different. Health was such a fragile gift. But Roby had been cheated of his whole life. I pictured him struggling with the chief or with Coño, and yelling for my dad before being thrown overboard. I punched the bulkhead.

"The chief is a dangerous man." Tomas's words echoed: I recalled the dread in his hushed, rasped tone and the wild, suffering eyes. Hell, look at me. I was lucky the chief hadn't killed me, as Gordo had said. I wanted to kill him…the bastard. Screw the police! If he was connected, he could come after me. But as far as the chief knew, he had killed me, or at least left me maimed.

What chance did I have? I wished I was a soldier. But I could fight. I thought of my boxing coach, the Marine; his shaven head. I resembled him now. Hell, I'd stood up to Coño and his brothers in the hold—three against one. I'd gotten this far on my own, on my wits. The chief wouldn't expect me to come after him, especially after the beating. That could be my edge. Surprise. I'd been drunk and careless in La Guaira. I'd dropped my guard. That wouldn't happen next time.

I went back to my cabin and opened my porthole. A paint-gun swished from the bow; a mist of paint dust floated in. Parallel to *Trader*, a massive red, blue, and yellow trolley-crane stood on high-capacity steel wheels that drove on heavy-duty rails the length of the graving dock. The red supports looked like giant crab-legs, the blue cab like the shell high above the legs, and the yellow boom and counter-weight like a single claw. Even without an operator, it looked alive. A second flanked the starboard side.

Beside *Trader* was a flooded and vacant basin. Beyond that, a floating drydock with a tugboat in a cradle. Sun-bleached tires hung from its gunwales. A forklift carted a gleaming bronze screw to mount on its naked shaft. The graving dock where *Trader* rested was in a narrow shipping canal in front of the main waterway. Across this canal, the inlet led to a quay that harbored a fleet of shrimp boats. An old wooden pier sagged on barnacle-covered pilings. From each trawler's aft mast, drag nets hung on runners. Hog-rings fastened the nets to the cables that opened like arms to the hot morning sun. Long booms towered vertically forty or fifty feet. A tow-cable ran from a block at the top of each boom down to the nets. All seven boats ranked and lashed together rolled in the wake of a tug boat coasting through the channel. Tires bumped and squeaked. The weight of the vertical booms rocked the boats. Blocks clanged and nets swayed. The trawlers probably ran back and forth between Curaçao and Venezuela to shrimp the coastal reefs.

Knuckles rapped my door. "Cesar, the captain wants to speak with you in his quarters." Chino delivered his summons and left. I knew what this was about—the report.

Because of the fever, the nurse, and the dentist, I'd managed to avoid McMorris for seven days. I dressed slowly. No way around this. I dragged down the passageway and slumped up the ladderway. His cabin door stood open and hooked to the bulkhead. He sat at the head of the table wearing his favorite Hawaiian shirt. Folded hands rested on the red and white checkerboard table cloth. His eyes were fixed on my face. I stopped at the opposite end of the long table already set for his breakfast. He remained silent.

"Guess this concerns the report, right sir?"

He nodded.

"Well, sir…I remember questioning the chief about my brother's disappearance. And…I guess…I insulted him. You know. Since he was the OOD that morning."

"Why didn't you write this down the first day?"

"I was still in shock and confused, sir."

He squinted and scratched his bald spot. "Go on."

"I basically called him incompetent for letting Roby fall overboard unnoticed. And he lost it, and exploded. That's really about it, sir."

"How 'bout Coño and his brothers?"

"Don't know, sir. Guess they stick together. But, of course, you're aware of the scuffle I had with them in the hold?"

"Yes, I know about that." He drew a long breath. "OK—that'll do for now. But your father's taking back command when we dock in Houston. We will reopen this topic at that time. For now, you're free to leave."

"Very well, sir." Half the truth was always better than a lie. Scrambled eggs always tasted better than hard-boiled and were a lot easier to scoop up than sunny-side-up or over-easy. Hell, by the time they hit the stomach, all eggs got scrambled anyway. McMorris liked his scrambled—at least for now. I turned to leave.

"By the way, Cesar."

I looked back. He still hadn't budged: hands folded and blue eyes fixed. "Yes, sir."

"I assume you're fit to start working again."

"Yes sir, I can start back on deck tomorrow."

"Tomorrow?" His eyes followed my hand as I rubbed my jaw. "All right, tomorrow then."

"Thank you sir." I rushed away from his scrutiny. I stayed in my cabin the rest of the day and snuck out after mealtimes to scrounge leftovers.

***

The next day, I waited 'til 0800 and joined the crew for breakfast instead of starting at 06 with the deck gang. I sat at my usual place, but avoided eye contact with Chino as he set the table. He worked silently, filling pitchers and placing silverware.

Soon after, Rafa and the carpenter came in. They didn't say much either, just a surprised hello, then an awkward pause as they scanned my stitches and bruises. El Indio and Simon joined us. They glanced at my face and quickly turned away. The Mexican oilers followed. The one who'd grabbed my arm at *Las Señoritas* tapped my shoulder as he passed and sat at the second table.

The servers brought in eggs, bacon, ham, potatoes, and the familiar white rice. Things were back to normal. We had a choice of apple juice or orange juice and several large pots of coffee. Gordo must have been in a good mood because he walked into the mess room with a large basket loaded with scratch-made biscuits. Everyone attacked and scooped up a fat, hot biscuit in each hand.

Finally, Tomas hurried in. He paused when he saw me and slid in next to me. Then he snatched up the last two biscuits and started buttering them. "Going to join us today?" he said and stuffed half a biscuit in his mouth; his buck teeth ripped into it.

I nodded and carefully bit down on a slice of bacon, avoiding conversation. They picked up on it and left me alone. I couldn't get my mind off the trawlers. Today was the ninth day in Curaçao. *Trader* would leave for Houston soon—a day more, maybe two at best. The brushing of red-lead was almost finished, and we could paint the holds at sea before reaching Houston. So what was left? "Rafa, do'you know when we leave?"

"If they deliver the new winch for holds three and four, and finish painting the hull, maybe late tomorrow," he said.

I nodded as though it wasn't important. But I scrunched my toes when he said it. The single most important thing…the one conviction I couldn't shake was that God, Fortune, Destiny, or whatever had put a great task before me. Let the chief go for now, file charges, and wait for the police; or track him down myself.

This was my test. Whatever the outcome, whatever course I chose, that choice would stand for me—my worth. The actions I took would be the yardstick to measure myself with—forever. It would define who I was. And my choice was tied to *Trader* and

Curaçao. Once she took to sea, my window for action would close. I had one day to hatch a plan.

After breakfast the deck gang split up. Tomas and Simon finished brushing No. 1 with red-lead. Rafa, El Indio, and the carpenter began dismantling the winch and sent me to retrieve a dolly from the forepeak. Within an hour, they'd removed the winch. We scraped the rusted skids and platform with steel brushes and coated the stripped metal with blood-colored primer. Then the three of them wrestled the winch onto the dolly and pushed it to the forepeak to be stowed for parts. Rafa told me to take it slow since it was my first day back; he didn't want me to tear my stitches.

It was almost lunchtime. The day was hot and sunny. A light breeze swept over the trawlers and across the inlet. I relaxed on the platform, leaned against the bulwarks, and watched the shrimp boats rock with the wake of passing boats. The nets still hung aft and the breeze carried a smell of sun-dried crustaceans.

On the trawler next to the pilings, three sailors lounged drinking beer. Two sat on a coil of manila line faked down between the stern's bitts; the third stretched out in a hammock beneath the nets. One of the black sailors on the coil lit a cigarette, took a long drag, and passed it to the sunburnt, knotty-haired blond who lay in the hammock. A sweet, fibrous odor drifted across the inlet—it was a joint. Huh…what if I paid them to take me across the bay to La Guaira? Would they do it? Cash was good bait. I still had the six hundred stashed in my cabin. Would that be enough?

The first obstacle was that McMorris still had my passport. I couldn't very well ask for it. And suppose the shrimper did agree to take me? I'd have to sneak away at night, before *Trader* shipped out—or I'd be discovered. And last, where would I stay once I reached La Guaira? The best place would be with Mia and Tomas's girlfriend. So, I'd need Tomas. But would he come?

During lunch, I began screwing with Tomas's head. I made sure I sat across from him. I stared at him and gnawed my food. It was easy to make ugly faces since chewing hurt. I glared deep into his eyes and used my fingers to eat. Once, I popped out the bottom partial and cleaned it with a napkin as he watched, blinking. "What's the matter with you?" he finally asked.

"Just thinking." I outweighed him by thirty pounds. My tactics were working; he started fidgeting with his food. Dropped his knife and had to wipe it clean. He took tiny sips of water and peeked at me over the rim of the glass. I looked straight at him each time. When the others left the table, I dropped the bomb. "I'm going to turn my official report in to the captain after dinner."

He gasped. "What are you saying?"

"You and I need to talk more before I write it up. I'm not convinced you've been honest with me."

"What? But…"

"Tonight, after dinner." I got up from the table and left him whining.

After lunch, we waited for delivery of the winch until 1800, but it never arrived. I was happy; that meant a delay. Also, the dock workers didn't finish painting the hull. Rafa said they were shorthanded. He estimated departure late on the eleventh day at 2300, since it required flooding the basin and easing her out.

Next, I had to carrot one of the shrimp boat captains. So after work, I waited until the officers and crewmen were eating. I skipped dinner and darted over the gangway.

I followed the U-shaped pier to the quay of trawlers across the narrow inlet. The planks of the old pier creaked as I jogged toward the shrimp boats. The bow lines were fastened to cleats and pilings. Midship the boats were lashed to each other and a few of the center ones had dropped anchor and passed long lines from the sterns to the pilings. The fishermen would cross from one to the next on shifty planks, or use a dinghy. Lobster traps were stacked on their fo'c'sle; the stench of shellfish infused the air.

Willemstad, Curaçao is the capital of the Netherlands Antilles, so I wasn't surprised that the fleet of shrimp boats all had Dutch names. I slowed my stride and read: *Holland's Pride, Commodore, Jan's Lot, Isabel's Lot, Martinus's Lot, Cornelia's Lot,* and the seventh one alongside the pilings—*Zeeman's Lot.* This last was where I'd watched the knotty-haired blond lounging on the hammock and smoking weed. I sauntered up and put my boot on the tire that hung from the gunwale. Rubber squeaked against the piling as it swayed. At high-tide, the trawler sat up level to the pier. The lanky blond still snored in the hammock. Beer cans crammed a five-gallon bucket beneath him. There was no one else aboard, so I put a little weight on the gunwale to rock her some. "Hey, man."

His head turned and he opened his eyes. Then he sat up in the hammock and dangled his legs out of each side. His beard was matted and tangled. A large black shark tooth hung from green monofilament around his neck, and the saw tooth cutting edge was snagged into his knotted, long blond hair. He rubbed his face with both hands. "Yeah. Who are you?" He had a thick Dutch accent. He crawled out of the hammock and staggered to a bait cooler, burrowed through the melting ice, and pulled out a beer. He popped the top and chugged it; foam dribbled down his mustache and into his beard. He took a breath and guzzled the rest. Then burped, crushed the can with one hand, mashed it flat between both his palms, and tossed the remains in the bucket. Aluminum clattered as his shot ricocheted inside. He slumped forward, clutched the shrimp net with one hand, and peered through the mesh at me. "What the hell you want?"

"When you going back out?"

"Why? You want to buy shrimp?"

"Maybe."

"Next full moon, when the tide goes out. I think...tomorrow."

"What if a guy wanted to get to La Guaira? Would you take him?"

"That's almost two hundred miles. Way out of our way."

"OK. How much would you need?"

"Shit, five hundred dollars at least. Or a thousand guilders."

"I have dollars. And I'll have a friend with me."

"Another two-fifty for your friend."

"Come on. A hundred."

"OK, I guess. Just don't drink all my beer. What happened to your face? You on the run?"

"No, just got beat up in a bar fight and stranded, and I have a girl in La Guaira. So, we have a deal for six hundred?"

"Not yet. Cash up front or no deal."

"You the skipper? It's your boat?"

"Yeah, this one's mine. Remember, cash."

"No problem. Tomorrow—then." I leaned over the side and shook his callused hand. That went a lot easier than I figured on, but six hundred...son of a bitch. All I had. He was probably headed that way anyhow, and I'd be paying for all his food, beer, and fuel. But timing was essential. And I still had to bully Tomas into going with me.

The Dutchman watched as I left, so I passed *Trader* and walked toward the main waterway. I waited fifteen or twenty minutes before I doubled back, sprinted across the gangway, and hustled to my cabin to wait for Tomas.

Not ten minutes passed before I heard his signature double knock. He was acting all humble-pie. I calmly closed the door behind him. He turned to face me.

I spun and gave him four quick upper cuts to the solar plexus. Right—left, right—left as hard as I could. He crumpled to his knees and wheezed. Then slithered down my leg and slumped to the deck as he held onto my ankle.

"Now, listen here, you son of a bitch. As far as I'm concerned you're as much to blame for my brother's death as the piece of shit that threw him overboard. I'm jumping on a shrimp boat tomorrow night and going after the bastard. You either come with me, or I'm telling McMorris and the owners everything I know. Then you can deal with the cops."

He lay on the deck clutching my ankle, sucking air. "The chief'll kill you," he muttered.

"That's my problem. Right? I need a place to stay in La Guaira—Tañía's. So you best be ready to go after dinner—clear?" I raised my fist as if I was going to hit him again. He held his hand out in front of his face and I lowered it. He stayed on his side coughing and gasping for another five minutes before he sat up against the bulkhead. "How much cash do you have?" I asked.

"What?"

"The shrimp boat captain wants six hundred US to take us to La Guaira. That's all I've got. So, how much do you have?"

"I can give you a hundred. I need the rest for my wife and kids back home," he mumbled.

"Don't fuck me over, Tomas. I've had enough bullshit. I'm not playing nice anymore. Understand?"

"Yeah . . . got it."

"Now remember. After dinner—tomorrow. Meet me here."

"I heard you." He staggered to his feet and left holding his gut.

I really didn't have anything to pack and wanted to go light. I sealed the money in a plastic baggie. But I needed more. The only person I could trust was Gordo. I could ask for a loan. I'd write a note telling Dad to reimburse him. He could hand it to the old man in Houston. Besides, I had to let Pop know something. So I found a sheet of paper.

Attn. Captain Santino
September 25
Curaçao

Dear Mom and Dad,

Mom, I promised I'd find out what happened to Roby. Though I don't know every detail, I do know, without a doubt, that he was murdered. I suspect he was clubbed, weighed down, and thrown overboard by Alejandro Larosa, the Chief Mate of the M/V Caribbean Trader.

Dad, the chief has been smuggling cocaine from Venezuela to US Ports (mainly Port Everglades) for some time. Roby saw a pickup in progress and was thrown overboard.

Secondly, when I found this out, the chief tried to kill me in La Guaira and then he jumped ship there. I WILL NOT LET HIM GET AWAY. Mom, I cannot and will not wait for the Lord, Karma, or the Law to catch up with him.

Dad, you've given me ships and the sea and these things made me a man. Mom, you've taught me to love and trust in the Lord. I can't say whether these things have led me to this choice, or if I'm turning away from them by choosing this path. I only know this is something I must do. I must try to set things right. I love you both as I love my brother Roby.

> *Your son,*
> *Cesar Santino*
> *PS: Gordo lent me_____. Please reimburse him.*

I left a blank for the amount and put the letter in an envelope without sealing it. I wrote *Attn. Captain Santino* on the front. Tomorrow after dinner, I'd give it to Gordo and ask for a loan. I sat up in my bunk searching for snags in my plan until I fell asleep.

***

The next day I worked with the deck gang. The drydock company delivered the winch after lunch and we had it bolted down, wired, and tested before 1800. Tomas ducked each time we made eye contact. I began to worry he might back out on me. But he showed up at my cabin at 1830, silent and humble, carrying a small duffel, and handed me a folded wad with a couple of fifties on the outside. I told him to sit tight and wait, that I had one thing left to do. I went to the galley with the letter in my back pocket.

Chino was cleaning up the officers' mess. I went down the ladderway. Rafa and the deck gang were drinking beer watching soccer in the crew's mess. I slipped into the galley. Gordo was washing pots. "Gordo, I need a loan."

"Cabron . . . how much?"

"Five hundred."

He raised both arms, dripping suds "Cabron, why so much?"

"Yes or no?"

"Until when?" He wiped his hands on the apron.

"My father will repay you. Listen, I'm leaving for La Guaira tonight. I'm going after the son of bitch who killed Roby and I need your help."

"Estas loco." He lowered his head.

"Maybe so, but that's what I'm doing. Will you help me?"

"No, I think you should go to the police. The chief is well connected in Venezuela. You won't get close to him." He stared at me and shook his head.

I thought for a moment. "Why? What else do you know?"

"Nothing. I told you that already. But it's risky. El Soldado has friends . . . many friends." I stared at him, silent. He finally gave in and wobbled out toward his cabin, leaving me standing in front of a hot stove. I surveyed the galley. Hanging from a hook was a heavy steel machete that had been ground down so many times it was shortened to a point like a sword and was as sharp as a fillet knife. He probably used it for cleaning fish.

When he returned, I hefted it. "I'm taking this with me."

"You really are crazy. Larosa's going to kill you. He's a professional soldier. He's killed many times." He handed me five hundred-dollar bills, still shaking his head.

I opened the letter, showed it to him, and wrote $600 in the blank spot. Then sealed it and gave it to him. "An extra hundred, for the favor. You're the only one I trust, Gordo. Give this to my father. Captain Santino will repay you."

He stared at me, mouth open. I turned to leave and heard him say, "Bicho malo nunca muere—an evil bug never dies."

My stomach tensed, I bit down on the partial, paused a moment, looked in his eyes, and gripped his big meaty sweat-drenched hand. "If I find him, this one will," I said.

When I returned to my cabin, Tomas squatted on the stool with both hands on his head, muttering a Padre Nuestro. "Say a prayer for me, too. Later, but now let's move," I said. The heavy, narrow machete had a leather string tied through a hole in the butt. I slipped a bread-tie through the leather string and wrapped it around a belt loop. The point reached my knee.

We snuck down the passageway to the shelter deck then down to the main deck and across the gangway. It was dark. The dockworkers swarmed the food vans at the far end of the pier. *Trader*'s hull glimmered in fresh red and blue. I'd timed it well. The workers would be back soon to begin flooding the graving dock and a tug would be here to lead her out.

We hurried around the creaky pier like escaped cons to the shrimp boat. The Dutch skipper lay in his hammock. Two shirtless, stocky black sailors sat cross-legged on manila coils. The trawler was secured with only a bow and stern line to the pilings. The skipper crawled out of the hammock when he saw me. "Was wondering if you'd show. Got it?"

"Yeah." I handed him exactly six hundred. The rest I'd stuffed in my pants. Maybe I should've held half, but if I haggled, and we argued, someone aboard *Trader* might hear. Best to move fast.

He counted it and said, "Climb aboard, mate." Then pressed a starter. The diesel roared. One of the sailors jumped from the stern to the wooden pier. He let loose the bight from that piling and tossed in the line. Then he sprinted to the bow and leaped back aboard with the bight in one hand, and we sputtered out through the inlet. Tomas squatted on a pin at the bitts, put both hands on his head, and stared at the deck. I gazed up at *Trader* as we passed her. She looked regal and untainted in a fresh coat of paint. She was bigger than life or death: the gunwales glossy black, the hull dark navy-blue down to the 30-foot draft mark and crimson-red from there to the keel. I was leaving a friend I might never see again.

The knotty-haired skipper throttled down when we reached the mouth of the channel. A wave crashed and foam covered the bow. The boat lifted and dropped into a trough. I grabbed a slimy shrimp net. Another wave bashed into us and the spray drifted over the deck. The cool breeze filled my lungs, moist and salty. The ocean was dark ahead. The sky was dim; channel lights and city lights glittered behind us. The deck rumbled beneath my boots. The breeze brought more briny mist and the trawler headed out.

17:
ZEEMAN'S LOT

Adim sapphire moon climbed the early night sky as the trawler *Zeeman's Lot* churned east-southeast from the mouth of Willemstad harbor. Out on the dark ocean the trade winds raised a swell. Every now and then she dropped into a trough, vibrated and clanged as spray engulfed the bow and sent a cool saline mist drifting across the decks. I let go the shrimp net that hung from the cross-section above and toppled back on my heels onto a hawser faked on the stern's spacious working-deck. The machete dangling from my belt banged into the manila coil as I sank into the center.

The full-moon was still low off the port side. A stout, shirtless black shrimper haunched down beside me. He followed my gaze. "It's blue because the westerlies bring the ash and smog down from Kīlauea and then across from Mexico or Colombia and over Venezuela." He spoke English with an eccentric twang; a blend of Papiamentu and Dutch.

"What's Kilauea?"

"Powerful volcano. In Hawaii. Erupted earlier dis 'ear."

"Drifts this far?"

He nodded and extended a large, warm hand. "Looks like something or someone blew up on you." He surveyed my stitched chin and slashed head. "They call me yu'i Korsou but my name is Colá."

"Why?"

"It means child of Curaçao." A large jagged scar creased his bare ribs and another mirrored it on his broad back. He bragged that a bull shark had nibbled on him while spear-fishing and boasted that he could free-dive two hundred feet on one breath. He reached into the cooler and pulled out three beers, gave me one, and threw the other to Tomas, who cracked the tab and started gulping it down. Big green letters read Grolsch, brewed in Holland.

"So what you running from? You're both off that bulk carrier—right?" Colá. smiled. Chipped white teeth gleamed in the moonlight framed by plump lips. He had salt-and-pepper hair and a puka-shell choker clasped around a stout neck. He stood up, on callused bare feet, swayed, and clutched the drag net. Then took a long slug of beer, pumped his hips, and started a rasped chant.

> *"You runnin, and you runnin, and you runnin away.*
> *But you can't run away from yourself. No-no-no-no."*

He cackled and sashayed two steps forward. Then guzzled back the rest, flipped the empty can into the bucket, and dug in the cooler for another. The trawler rattled against the crashing chop; the skipper slowed the engine. The next crest sent the beer-can bucket skating on the deck. Colá snatched it and lodged it inside the coil on the starboard side. The second sailor grabbed two beers from the jam-packed cooler then scaled the

151

slimy deck toward the fo'c'sle. He tossed one to the skipper as he slipped by the wheelhouse and lashed down a lobster trap that was battering at the gunwales.

I ignored the question, lurched to my feet, and clutched the low side when she dipped into the next trough. The trawler's deep hull and a wide beam kept her stable despite the towering outriggers. Above, the towing-blocks glimmered in the running-lights. They rattled and clattered and clanged as she tussled with the sea. Tomas stayed aft by the bitts and stared at the deck. He lifted his head, timed a sip of beer between a pitch and a roll, then fixed his gaze down again.

I slid forward along the narrow companionway. The gunwales, low across the beam, sheered up to the cabin and wheelhouse. The sliding door was open and the knotty-haired skipper gripped the small steel helm. I stopped in front of the wheel and glanced at the compass: 113 ° ESE. He looked me over. "Don't worry; I'll take you to La Guaira."

"Just checking."

"We're going to drag through Golfo de Triste outside Puerto Cabello after I drop you two. This old tub's equipped with freezers."

"How long?"

"Well, we're doing about ten knots, so…around twenty hours—with good seas. What's your name again?"

"Does it matter?" I stepped to the starboard doorway and gazed back at the fading lights of Curaçao. Had anyone aboard *Trader* noticed our getaway?

"All right, don't tell me. Mine's Dirk. I was born in Amsterdam. My uncle owns most of those trawlers back in Willemstad but he's getting old now. He rarely goes out any more and stays drunk most nights. During World War Two, merchant sailors on the Murmansk run. My granddad drowned."

"Sorry to hear"

"Ah, don't care. Don't remember him. Not even a tadpole then."

The trawler rolled off a wave. We were in the ocean now; the harbor lights mere flickers. Deep wide swells lifted and rocked her. As she fell into a trough, a wave broke against the bow and drenched the bridge's large windows.

The sailor clambered down off the poop deck. He stopped beside the portside doorway and pointed. "Schipper, luke." Against a dark ocean, the moonlight revealed a thrashing burst of white spray two hundred yards from us.

The long-haired Dutchman rose to his toes. "Let's take a look." He turned the wheel hard to port and approached the mass. "Looks like a whale carcass…and plenty of sharks feeding." The murky sea camouflaged several large dorsal fins. They shimmered in the moonlight and dove beneath the waves. A massive and segmented white belly floated, corralled by a school of white-tipped dorsal fins and three large, darker fins that slashed through the circle. One rammed and mauled the bloated meat, then thrashed the water and vanished. Another took its place while the smaller sharks darted at the sinking chunks. "The big ones look like tigers; the white-tips are the oceanic, but they stay clear of those tigers." He circled while Colá and Tomas gawked from the stern, then resumed our heading. "Not smart to stay here. A big one might slam the boat."

"Hell no! Make way," I said. He tapped down on the throttle and we rumbled off.

"That's the worst way to go, ripped to shreds and still alive. Better to sink and drown," he said.

"I'd rather die old on a farm-house porch dreaming in a rocking chair," I said.

"Not most sailors' fate."

"No, I reckon not, maybe a beach-house porch then," I said.

He raised his eyes from the lubber's line and grinned. "My uncle's told me lots of stories about sailors who died at sea. That's how I named the boat—*Zeeman's Lot.*"

"Oh…that's what it means."

"Some run aground like the *Amsterdam* in 1749. In the wars many were torpedoed . . . like the German battleship *Bismarck*. *Provence*, a French ship, sank with 3100 sailors….Of course, there's *Titanic*—1500 drowned in ice water. And who knows how many ships and sailors rest on Iron Bottom Sound in the Solomons?"

"My old man told me his Spanish cousin had a bulk carrier go down with all hands."

"Bet a lot of those swabbies wished they'd never sworn out the Sailor's Creed." He glanced into my eyes, then reached for his beer, perched in a cup holder mounted to the side of the steering unit. "But that's how it is; sooner or later…you have to swim for your life." He studied my eyes again. "Go back and get me another beer…sailor."

I didn't like him, but it was his boat. I nodded, ambled out of the wheelhouse, and slithered down the narrow deck between the cabin-house and the gunwales. I gripped the handrail then clutched the gunwale the last few slippery steps and went for the cooler.

"How 'bout those fooking sharks," Colá said.

154

"Santo de Dios." Tomas made the sign of the cross on his forehead.

"Those are the real masters out here." Colá gazed over the stern.

"Bosses of the deep," the other black sailor said as he slid by me. He mumbled some foreign syllables and plumped down beside the cooler.

I grabbed another beer, turned and waddled a few steps, then clasped the railing back to the wheelhouse. I stepped inside and handed it to Dirk.

"Dank u."

"I'm going to stretch out and close my eyes." I glanced at the compass again and moved out of the wheelhouse. I clenched the railing back to the stern, balancing my beer, and sank into the hawser. The cloudy sky veiled the stars but the full moon peeked through at times. The breeze filled my lungs. The choppy sea bashed the bow and threw back a blanket of briny mist. Nestled into the manila, I savored my cold beer.

Tomas was silent. I didn't care. I closed my eyes. Colá and the other sailor chattered on in Papiamentu. The African-sounding melody filled my ears and I fell asleep.

***

Hours later, a wave clattered the blocks and tackle. I woke, stumbled to the wheelhouse, and checked the compass again. Still ESE. Colá stood at a window and studied the waters ahead. Dirk was still welded to the wheel. We exchanged muffled 'hellos' and I returned aft where Tomas snored on the portside hawser. I wedged back into my spot and closed my eyes again.

The next time I opened them, Tomas stood with knees lodged beneath the gunwales balancing a long and clumsy piss. The trawler rolled to lee, then back. He cussed and clutched the side to keep from going over, then zipped up and lay down again. I floundered to the side, bobbed out a ham-fisted piss, then lunged back to my hempen nest.

***

The bright morning glare warmed my face. I sat up on the coil to contemplate the white-capped sea. The waves still battered us, heeling us to port. Spray slapped my face. I wiped off cheeks and forehead then the back of my neck and mulled over the choice I'd made jumping ship. What would McMorris do? Should I have left him a note as well? The salt parched my lips and singed my lacerations.

When the day heated up, I went inside the wheelhouse. Tomas didn't speak much English and Antilleans didn't like to speak Spanish, so he kept drinking beer sprawled out beneath the swaying drag-nets that filtered the hot sun. The northeasterly picked up and rattled *Lot;* the Caribbean rolled and pitched her.

In the wheelhouse, Colá struggled with the helm. He had a wide stance and the veins in his neck and arms filled with blood each time he pushed on a spoke to keep our course. He seemed larger and stronger at the wheel. He glanced at me. "Skipper rests now. You want to check the course, go ahead. We're running southeast by east and later today we'll turn southeast." He grinned and flexed his chest then glanced back at the line. "Skipper said you'd come by to check." He smiled again.

His grin bothered me. It seemed to hold a secret I was ignorant of. I checked the damn compass—124°. Never ignore the obvious; I'd learned that boxing. I leaned against the bulkhead by the starboard glass and gazed at white-blotched emerald sea. Several ships dotted the horizon. But they stood far away from *Lot*.

Mid-day, Dirk piled in carrying cans of sardines, a box of crackers, and two beers. He gave Colá a beer and passed out the food. I was hungry, but too dehydrated to eat. I wanted water. I took the sardines and went aft to the recycle bucket, grabbed an empty can, and filled it with melted ice-water from the bottom of the cooler. The ice-cold liquid tasted dirty but dropped my body heat like a soothing river. I ate the salty sardines, drank more water, and stayed aft. Tomas started drinking beer again and pissing and then drank another.

The afternoon dragged on. The wind never let up and the seas stayed choppy but not too rough—five-to-six. Seagulls joined us near dusk and I knew we were close. I checked the heading—SE 136°.

The sun slowly descended like a great orange yolk and gradually stretched out on the flat-pan horizon. It sank from a red-orange ball to a semi-circle to a long tangerine line that meshed the darkening sea to the pale blue sky. Moments later, only pink shades remained west, and southeast the lights of Puerto La Guaira began to flicker into view. First, the glow of the port, then behind it, city lights flashed on the mountainside like candles. Sheets of spray towered from the bow half way up the outriggers. Gulls circled, screeching.

Through the wheelhouse's back window, I noticed the heads of the crew huddled in the center. It looked like a heated conversation. It reminded me of the chief and the Mexicans. I watched a moment longer and moved in low behind the cabin-house. But I couldn't hear them. So, I went up to the doorway. When I came through, they separated leaving Dirk behind the wheel. "Everything OK?" I said.

"Yeah. We're getting close," Colá said.

"Thought so."

"Yeah…and we're worried about patrol boats. You're both a.w.o.l.—right? Do you have passports?" I shook my head. Dirk stood up behind the wheel and glanced at the compass. "There's a long jetty a mile or so from the port…close to the hotels. It forms a breakwater for the beaches. Several reefs border it. That's the best spot to swim for."

"Swim?" I said.

He tapped down on the throttle. "Yeah…goofball. I told you—zeeman's lot."

"What? How far?"

"Not sure yet. We'll see."

Colá moved past him through a narrow companionway into the chart room and walked back in with a sawed-off double-barreled. The sailor behind him wore a black holster clipped to his belt, sheathing a wooden-handled, nickel-plated snub-nose.

"What the hell's this?" I said.

"Just in case you get stupid with that machete you've got there. So drop it on the deck." I untied it from my belt and let it fall. Dirk kicked the blade against the bulkhead. It clanged and slid to the corner.

At that point, Tomas staggered onto the bridge. "Cabrones, porque las pistolas?" He put his arms in the air as if we were in some spaghetti western. The trawler rolled and he braced against the front window.

"I'll get as close as possible, but where I say, you two are in the drink. Got it?" Dirk glared at me then at Tomas.

"How about a raft? Damn. Come on, man," I said.

Colá poked at me with the shotgun. I backed into a corner and kept silent after that. And for the first time since I'd punched the breath out of him back in Curaçao, Tomas sought my company. He stumbled over. "What's happening?" he slurred.

"We have to swim for it."

"I'm a little drunk. How far?" He started pinching his bottom lip into one of his buck-teeth and contorting his beer-breath mouth. "How about sharks?" He rushed through the sign of the cross several times.

"I know, I know…but what choice do we have." We turned to watch our captors. The sailors stood together like MPs guarding prisoners: Colá with the sawed-off in both hands pointing down at the deck and the other bastard with his hand on the holstered revolver. Dirk steered, eyeballing me between glances at the lubber's line. Through the windows, the lights were getting closer. Tomas looked worried; I was, too. "Listen, Dirk. He's been drinking. You've got to get closer in. A lot closer than this."

"Shut up. You're lucky we don't take all your money," Dirk said.

"We're not thieves," Colá added. "We just don't want to get boarded and searched."

We stood in silence, balancing and staring across the wheelhouse at the armed sailors who stared back at us. Maybe they had contraband; drugs or stolen merchandise aboard. Otherwise, why the guns? The blocks and tackle rattled above. The nets swayed. Dirk steered the course.

After what seemed like hours, he sighed, "OK, this is it." He told the sailor with the snubnose to take the helm, and pulled it from its sheath. "Both of you out on deck." He wagged the shiny steel at me and we backed out of the wheelhouse and staggered aft. They followed with one hand gripping the rail, the others pointing the guns. When I looked toward the shore the lights didn't seem far, but the sea was murky with a light chop. "Keep moving," Dirk said.

"Come on, man. Get us closer."

"Fuck you. You're going in here. Alive or dead. Your choice." They pointed their weapons at the sea. "Move."

"How 'bout life-preservers, floats. Anything." I tried to stall the inevitable.

"Colá, get them something—without our name on it." He left and returned with two worn-out, scuffed and ripped life jackets. I sighed and put one on, then helped my sobering comrade with his.

"OK, now over before we get spotted." They nudged us to the lowest point midship and prodded us over like pirate victims forced to walk the plank.

I tensed, took a breath, and plunged in. The water was warm. I started propelling upward and couldn't. Forced one boot off and then the other. Socks were next. I floated. Thank God…I floated. I bobbed in the sea and looked for Tomas. He came up spitting. Dirk and Colá leaned over and looked down, smiling. "Good luck," Colá said.

"Fuck you," I yelled back. He pointed the shotgun down at me and grinned.

"Do the back-stroke," Dirk yelled and laughed.

"How far?" I yelled back.

"A couple miles. Now you're real sailors," Dirk called as *Zeeman's Lot* drifted out of reach.

"A couple miles?" I yelled and slapped the water. A wave smothered me. I wiped my face. "You bastard! You-son-of-a-bitch!" The other sailor reached behind him and threw me a beer. It hit the water and disappeared.

I turned and started swimming toward the lights. The waves were gentle rollers. I was grateful for that. The night was partly cloudy and the stars and moon took turns lighting the shadowy sea.

Swimming seemed futile; the lights didn't get any closer. But I kept at it. After a short while, Tomas started panting and spitting. Moments later it turned to gasping and coughing, and he vomited trails of foam.

Another hour passed and Tomas stopped swimming, and bobbed. He quit kicking his legs and barely used his arms. A wave covered him. I yanked his sleeve and yelled at him, "Don't give up. Keep swimming. Keep swimming!" I slapped water at his face. He turned on his back and tried the back-stroke for a while. So did I. My legs were dead, heavy. I stayed close and kept yelling at him, but it was as much for me as for him. Every so often I'd roar at him, thinking of a heavy bag and my coach screaming 'Snap that left in there." And I'd fling out an arm and yank back another stroke.

I stayed on task. Tried not to think about sharks, but now and then I couldn't help picturing the frenzied tigers back at the whale carcass. I'd stop swimming, tread water, and scrutinize the waves around me. "This is just a workout," I screamed. "Keep pushing." I'd tread water. Check Tomas. Check direction. Scan for lights. Scan for dorsal fins. Then resume swimming.

A long time passed doing the same things over and over. My thighs ached and kicking became a painful yet numb reflex. My fingers were shrivelled; lips and throat dry, salty. I sensed we gained way. The lights seemed closer. The closest was a flashing beacon. My pants were heavy, baggy. I swam toward the light, steering and pulling Tomas by his life-jacket. Soon, the water didn't seem as dark. I was tired but saw white water breaking on the shoreline. I pushed on.

We were close, a hundred yards from the rocks, when the moonlight gleamed on a small dorsal in front of us. Terror gripped me. Images of tearing jaws filled my thoughts. I didn't tell Tomas and kept a steady stroke. Didn't want to splash like bait. If it was a bull, it might attack anyway.

Next time I saw it, it was close, a car's length. The moonlight revealed a brownish fin. A sand shark? Maybe a bull? We were near the rocks. My toes touched the bottom as it came at me, sinking its jaws into the life preserver. A burst of air. White jaws thrashed. Its eyes rolled shut. Tomas screamed. Teeth lodged into the preserver and ripped it from me, then splashed away, shaking and gnawing its prize. We hurtled through the water like bait fish tangled in a net.

When we reached the rocks, a light shower started. We crawled along on our hands and knees and tumbled with each crash of the surf. Barnacles sliced my bare feet. My shoulder and arm bled from the force of the jaws ripping away the life jacket. My knees banged against the jagged mossy rocks. The breaking waves battered and pushed us along the long row of boulders. It was a relief to touch a solid object beneath me. From now on I'd trust no one. I had to control the situation—somehow. How else could I catch the damn chief?

The waves shoved us into a shallow pool leeside of a small cavern made by years of pounding waves. We lay there a long while, spitting and coughing and taking deep breaths. Tomas coughed convulsively then vomited again. I was nauseated and weak. I listened to the sea bashing the jetty and instead of thanking God, I yelled out, "Am I stupid?" That's what Colá's shit-eating grin had been all about. How many times had that jerk Dutchman told me, "Sooner or later every sailor has to swim for his life?" Couldn't I see it coming? Again I'd let my guard down.

We lay on our backs in the shallow pool, pummeled by the crashing surf. I stared up at the stars christened by the soft rain and remembered one of my ethics classes back at the university . . . and Machiavelli's words: "It is necessary…to learn how not to be good, and to use this knowledge and not use it, according to the necessity of the case."

18:
BURNING IN THE BARRIOS

We stuffed the life jackets between the breakwater-boulders, then stumbled along barefoot toward the shoreline. The rocks came straight out perpendicular to the shore. The coastline in front of the hotels was also piled with giant boulders to form a levee. We shuffled along the barnacled stones, cautiously planting our slashed and wrinkled feet, then over the levee and onto the sandy beach. I pulled off my soggy shirt, furiously squeezed and twisted it until I could wring out no more of the sea we had so narrowly escaped, then put it back on. Jeans hung drenched and low on our hips. Knees and thighs were scuffed slimy-green. Our feet were shrivelled, anemic, and bloodied.

Tomas wrung out his shirt and wrestled it back on. He leaned over, put each hand on a kneecap, and locked both arms. "We almost drowned."

"That asshole could've given us a raft," I said.

"I drank too much. You saved me." He held out a hand and stood.

I clasped it. "Help me find the chief."

"Tañía first," he said. He stretched forward, and slapped his plump beer-belly. He stumbled on, muttering, "Padre Nuestro, que estas en el cielo." then turned back and said, "This way."

The row of hotels lit up the shoreline. Drums and maracas trickled from a poolside party. Ripples sloshed up the creamy sand. I squished my toes and scored heels in the moist, soothing texture, brown like Mia's skin. Foam fizzled like seltzer as it receded over the bits of tan and yellow shells scattered along the water's edge. Windward, rolling thuds blasted sheets of white water overhead that splattered and glistened on the dark rocks like weighty sleet.

Every hotel had an outcropping of boulders that served as the seaside property line and a buttress against the sea. We waddled along at first, then began a measured stride; two soldiers in formation. Tomas called out the name of a hotel, if he remembered it, or if he saw a sign. With each his pace quickened. Lined up in ranks of two, beach-loungers and chairs faced the ocean behind thatched cabañas and tiki bars. Breakers surged in up to our ankles. The foam nipped at my cuts, then hissed and glided away.

After a mile or so, we scurried through the poolside patios of the Hotel Nacional and out onto the autopista, Avenida Soubelette again, but miles east of the port and even east of the main Plaza. We set forth on a long barefoot hike on dirty streets and sidewalks.

To the south and southwest, the hillsides were entrenched with winding red-clay dirt roads. Mud streets rose from the autopista into ghetto neighborhoods with grimy, flat dirty aqua blues and dingy pink apartment houses and bodegas; some with graffiti, others peeling and abandoned. Tomas pointed up the hillside. "They're burning. They're burning in barrios."

Halfway up a central knoll, on two ends of a dirt road, fireballs flared in the shadowy street. Each intersection had untamed demonstrations. Dark silhouettes packed together chanting around bonfires. We stopped and gawked. Revelers raised tires over their heads and flung them onto blazing stacks of pallets and branches. Some threw bottles at the raging infernos that blocked the roadway. The fire soared higher and the chanting grew louder, hands were raised, and the crowd began jumping up on their toes like wild bushmen.

"Why the burning?"

"Protestas y vendettas, o fiestas—quien sabe."

Black smoke spewed from the flames, permeating the night air with rubber and scorched wood. Soon sirens filled our ears and blue lights bustled up the muddy clay streets. We darted away like fleeing coyotes down the sidewalk screened by rows of areca palms and coconut palms that lined the easement alongside the autopista. Wet jeans were rolled up above our calves as we jogged barefoot on the coarse concrete sidewalk, my eyes fixed on the hillside fires and the bedlam.

I stopped. "Tomas, where are we going? The club?"

He turned and nodded.

"What if the chief's there? We can't just waltz in without a plan."

"Well, Tañía lives up around those fires. Would you rather go there?"

"Yeah—I would," I jabbed back.

"Well, what if they are home?" He smiled. "They might be working. They're whores, you know."

"Better than walking in on the chief and his traficante buddies without a plan."

"What if we get in a fight with the johns?"

"That's OK. After that Dutchman, I'm in the mood." I snapped a crisp left-right combination deep into his arm and shoulder.

He toppled back a step, rubbed the spot, turned, and cut through the areca palms to the highway. "Then this way— campion," he said. I followed, careful not to step on glass or sharp stones.

We dashed across a double lane onto the center island that divided the autopista. Three-story tall royal palms landscaped inside the parched grass boundary. Above us, the long fronds flapped with the breeze as though waving hello. We pranced over the opposing lanes and onto the opposite sidewalk. "What time is it?" he said.

I checked Roby's watch; it had stopped. I shook my head. "Must have banged it on the boulders." We walked to the first side street and headed up the clay road toward the rising smoke. I kept fidgeting with the watch trying to get it going but failed. I gave up and stuck it in a pocket. An odd gloominess settled in knowing Roby's watch wasn't ticking. I trudged on a step behind Tomas.

We veered around the bonfires into the shadows of narrow callejóns—alleyways. Sometimes, Tomas stopped and stared down a moonlit fork, then backtracked and led us up a better path. Soon our soles dragged heavy with mud. Children peered through glassless windows from adobe-brick buildings. I scanned the narrow lanes with dark porches up close to the edge of the tight roadway. Dogs barked; some rushed us, stopped a few feet away, snarled and snapped, but we kept a steady gait. We posed no threat, and they let us by.

Outside a bodega, three middle-aged women stood drinking and smoking cigarettes. They wore stretched bright red or yellow shorts and low cut blouses. The two heavyset ones hooted and waved as we trekked by; we stayed on the shoulder and kept quiet. After a few steps, Tomas nudged me. "These street putas . . . if they don't know you, they get you drunk, or in alley, and get their pimps to slash your thighs and rob you," he whispered. I looked back at the wide, endearing smiles. The two plump ones pulled down their blouses and jiggled brown breasts as I stared.

The third one, gaunt and bony, embraced a teenage girl who stood beside her—a last stab. "Mira...la niña...la niña linda," she yelled out. The girl, solemn and compliant, reclined in the slut's scrawny arms, eyes lethargic.

"Some sell their daughters, too," Tomas said. I dropped my eyes to the blood-muddy road and thought again of how the weak are quarried by the filth who exercise power over them.

The next murky lane hosted eight or nine adolescent ruffians bunched in front of a five-story emerald-green tenement with spotlights glaring down from the corners. Hundreds of moths circled the lights. Shouting blared out from a hallway like trumpets and horns. Bullet holes riveted a brick outhouse with red letters across the side wall that read Viva El Che.

The band of hooligans circled us as we approached. Tomas quickened his stride and skated past the closing arc; I slowed and raised my arms in a boxing stance. They were teenagers, but two or three had some meat on them, and a short, buffed, mestizo-looking kid carried a bright red and green stick-ball bat. He waved it at me. "Buscas niñas? Mota? Coca?"

"No nada," I said and tried to slip by, but one of the larger kids blocked my way. He shoved me. My arms were up, so I faked a left at his face and bitch-slapped him hard with my right. White-green snot shot from his nostrils; he winced away. A second pulled a blade and stepped toward me. I tightened up, raised my arms again and sidestepped away. A loud whistle came from the tenement house. Without looking back, the punk closed the knife, and the gang opened to let us pass.

In front of the building, two middle-aged men were playing dominos on a card table. A moth covered spotlight showered light on their game. They had a cooler beside them and lounged in old sofa chairs. From the open window above their heads, a radio purred merengue. The one who'd whistled stooped over the table; the swarm of moths circled the lamp high above his head like a halo. Once the gang resumed its post, he plunked back into his cushioned seat, leaned over the armrest and snagged two beers from the open cooler topped with ice and bottlenecks. He handed one to his opponent then grabbed a can of bug-spray off the window sill, misted the air around them, and resumed the game.

Tomas had stopped to watch from a few safe yards ahead. "Estas loco?" he said. I didn't even look at him, just marched by. He jogged to catch me. "I would've helped you…I would've." I kept hiking. "There was nine of them, you crazy Cuban."

"They were teenagers—yegua," I said.

"I'm no pussy." He punched my shoulder. I returned a stiff one-two. He screeched and pouted, then shook out and rubbed his arm. "You've got heavy hands," he muttered. I trudged on. He paused a moment longer massaging, then charged with his head out in front ready to tackle me. I pitched all my weight forward, met the charge, and stood him up with a forearm to the gut like a linebacker does a guard. Then I hurled him around me and into the mud.

He lay there, caught his breath, grunted, rose, and charged again. He let out a great bear-like roar as he dove at my knees. I spread my legs in a wide stance and buried his face in the mud.

He didn't have a chance. I was twice his size and in better shape. But he was pigheaded—had to respect that. He wiped the mud from his mouth and nose then spat and blew out, holding one nostril then the other. I laughed. He jumped up, coughed, and bulled in again. I shuffled back and one foot slid in a puddle. He rammed into me, bear-hugged my waist and we flipped over into the mud. My back hit with a splat. Still laughing, I slipped out from underneath and reversed our positions.

He coughed and quit, staring into my eyes with his hair in the mud. "I'm not a guerrero like you, but I'm not pussy." I smiled at him as a group of kids began clapping from a second story balcony. A terrier yapped at us; its head through the railing.

A bottle splattered a few feet away and rolled without breaking. Someone screamed out, "Borrachos." I helped Tomas up. We brushed and wiped each other's back, which only smeared worse, then rambled off, cackling like the winners of a rumble.

Shouting continued yards behind us. We sprinted up the red clay toward a level area. The road widened around a parroquia, a circular park. In the center, a small white clay basin was encircled by a radius of dark cobblestones. A white cross rose from the center of the shallow bowl. As we passed, several older women huddled in a cowering bunch. Each dipped a hand, twitched fingers back and forth on their foreheads, and moved on mumbling into the shadows.

After the blessed square, I looked back at the fires ensnared with flashing blue lights. Tomas led me to a building whose front wall looked like the Alamo. The arch-framed glass read *Bodega y Ferretrria y Pescado* in large white letters. "Tañía lives on the second floor," he said. We skimmed by the dimly lit entrance; the store was wide and deep, and several customers stood at the register carrying packages. The building's exterior wall was of red brick, one of the few I'd seen. An old Aztec or Mayan woman rocked in a chair on the front porch and gazed at the dark streets. She lifted a hand in silence as we passed.

I followed Tomas around back into a black, narrow lane for garbage cans. At the far end, a single staircase led up creaky, wooden steps to a row of rooms. The girls had the one on the end.

Tomas tapped twice. We wiped our faces and knocked mud off our knees. A bolt clunked. Then a latch rattled and the door opened. Tiny Mia stood barefoot with burgundy-red painted nails and a long white t-shirt that reached her knees. Her curly black hair was pulled back and tied with a pink scrunchie. "Tomas, Tomas," she screamed and jumped into his arms. He hugged her and asked for Tañía. "Trabajando, trabajando," she said. She turned to me, stared, then flung herself into my arms crying, "Cesar, Cesar... estas vivo, estas vivo." She kissed my shaved head hysterically, then pecked soft wet lips on the stitches still in my chin. She trembled. It took me by surprise. I didn't expect this burning affection. I felt like Odysseus returning home scarred and sea-scorched to Penelope's arms.

She pulled me and Tomas inside, latched and bolted, then catapulted into my arms again. The mud on my face meshed with her tears and smudged both our faces. She must have thought I was dead when they'd carted me out to the ambulance. She was only nineteen. But it was more than that. It was about how she'd felt that night sitting on my lap before the fight. To her, I was a Yanqui . . . .from a different world . . . a better place that I could sweep her off to.

Tomas finally got tired of watching the hugging and pampering. He stood. "Well, I'm going to *Las Señoritas* to see Tañía and leave you two alone."

"Wait a minute. How 'bout the chief?" I said, then turned to Mia. "Is El Soldado still around? You know—the tough guy I fought."

"No, no . . . se fue. Coño y sus hermanos también." She turned to Tomas. "En la bodega, hay teléfono para llamar un taxi." Tomas nodded and stood by the door until Mia unlocked it and let him out. She locked it again and leaned back against the door still holding the knob. She raised gleaming brown eyes, smiling like a little girl who's trapped a rare butterfly. Then she let go the knob, yanked off her t-shirt, and leaped naked into my arms.

I fell to the floor with the chocolate bon-bon on top of me. She ripped off my salty and muddy shirt and pulled loose my belt. Soon I was naked, hard, and smelled like crap. Giggling, she led me to the shower. She stepped in, grabbed a soap bar, and tugged at me. I gasped. The icy water took my breath away and half my hard. She began washing me like a slave girl bathing her master. She stuck hands and the soap bar everywhere—didn't even bat an eye. After a thorough swabbing, she knelt and sucked me off. Then stood, kissed my lips, and led me to the bed.

I slapped her ass and fucked her for hours. I didn't even think about protection. She didn't seem like a prostitute, just a young girl trying to survive in the predatory world she'd been dropped into. I remembered how some of the boxers around the gym used to say, "Treat a lady like a whore and she'll want you forever." But I knew where they'd heard that quote. The other half says, "...and treat a whore like a lady." Mia was no

172

lady, but she wasn't a whore either. She was swirling at the rim of an ocean-sized cesspool, and I was a sailor.

19:
PUTAS y NIÑAS

After things settled down, Mia nestled her head onto my chest and fell asleep with a smooth thigh wrapped over my leg. She drooled a little and made petite snoring noises like a warm, well fed infant snuggled in a blanket. I glanced around the bedroom for the first time now that the auburn filly was burned out and tamed down.

No windows, just a dresser, a mirror, and a double bed on a warped tongue-and-groove floor. The outside wall behind the bed was Spanish-style brick, and solid. A black dress draped in clear plastic hung on one side of the doorless closet; three or four bright paisley blouses hung on the other. Jeans were folded and stacked next to a mound of elfin slippers and dainty shoes that matched the blouses. On the dark, scuffed, wooden dresser, and shoved into the gap between the mirror and the frame, was a crinkled portrait-size photo of a family: two young girls, a mother, and a father. It was taped on two corners to the mirror at Mia's eyelevel. There were no drugs, or beer cans, or even cigarette butts. Hell, for what it was, the room looked clean.

Though the steadfast brick muffled the street noise, the interior walls were cardboard, or at best balsa. Voices seeped through like apparitions in the dark. Bouts of screaming bled from the adjacent room. A fit of frenzied laughter oozed up from the bodega through the twisted floorboards. A gun cracked in the street, a second bullet pinged off metal, then a third shot ricocheted into glass out in the back alley. Heavy steps scrambled below, accompanied by agitated murmurs. And of course, the staple of the streets—like white rice aboard *Trader*— the loyal barking of dogs and blaring sirens soon to follow. Howls and shrills resonated from the crimson-clay roads.

Then glass shattered next door and a fist-fight broke out between the man and the woman: slaps and shrieks. He yelled, "Puta!"

She hollered, "Borracho!" Then a crash and a thump, followed by whimpering. A door slammed, followed by a girl's frantic whining. Thuds and bangs engulfed the feral night like chipping-hammers cleaning rust, and the rust was the omnipresent crime and prostitution, and a general state of want fuelled by the drug-jones, like the depleted mud *Trader* brought fertilizer for, then smuggled back to the states, the very source of the problem. What a contrast from the ship, the sea, and the wind: bashing waves, the shrill of the ocean-breeze in my ear, salt spray stinging my face—the natural world. The barrios were a war zone—a different kind of war; without victors, without exit. This ubiquitous muck tarnished and smeared everything around it, but it also averted attention from me. This was a good place to lam out, gather intel, lay low, and plan my next move.

Mia purred, glued to my side, oblivious. Now and then, if the crash or shout was loud enough, she'd jolt and burrow closer. How could a young girl flourish in this quagmire? I thought back to the merriment of the college-sisters on sorority row; the dimpled blond with emerald-green eyes; the new students bragging about who they were going to be; the party I'd missed. Then the teen-girl boosted by the gaunt slut's arms seeped back in; the acquiescent, heart-rending lazy gaze in her eyes and the droop in her limbs.

Another hour passed. I thought about the chief, Coño and his brothers, the damn Dutchman and *Zeeman's Lot*, the fight with the Mexicans in the hold; the beating I'd gotten from the chief at the strip-club, the tigers...and how we could've drowned. I thought back to Mom's house and Roby's photo next to the flickering candles . . . and my promise to find out what had happened to him.

A thump-thump sounded on the door. Tomas. I shook Mia. "Que pasa, Papi," she whispered and kissed my chest. Girls giggled, followed by more knocks. Mia jumped up and pulled on a white t-shirt. In a scurry of little steps like a ballerina's, she dashed to unlock it, leaving a slit with a view of the apartment's entrance. I popped out of bed and into my still-damp boxers, reached into my jeans with the stashed roll of bills and stuck the money inside my pillow-case; Popeye, the sailor-man, looked up at me. On the other side of the bed, her pillow-case was a caricature of Olive Oyl. I grinned, jumped back on the bed, held the money inside Popeye and tucked the pillow behind my head. I sat up to scrutinize the inebriated assembly staggering in.

Tañía swayed in heels and a string-like outfit with rhinestone-studded strands and straps covering nipples, crotch, and butt-hole. Tomas had one arm around her neck and shoulders; she had one arm around his waist. Next, two floozies trampled in. I recognized the prettier from the club; she'd been with Coño the night of the fight. Last, a slim and nervous Colombian paused in the doorway, scanned the alley, then the street, glanced at the front room, stepped in, locked and latched the door. He didn't see me.

Mia said a quick "hola" and bolted back to the bedroom, shut the door, and leaped onto the bunk. She nestled up to me, kissed my chest, and grabbed my nuts. I pulled her hand away, stood, and pulled on my muddy jeans. Then crept up to the bedroom door and listened. I heard Tanía plop drunken-Tomas into her bed, batter the door closed, and rejoin her friends.

Mia pouted and sat up. She grabbed Popeye to cushion her back against the brick wall and the money dropped out. I turned and stomped to the bed, snatched it up, rolled the bills, and jammed them into my pocket. I glared into her eyes. She flushed. "Sorry, Papi."

The scene was heating up in the front room: loud laughing and wrestling. I had to take a piss, so I opened the door and stepped out, shirtless in my nasty jeans. The Columbian sprang up from the couch like a cobra and brandished a Glock in my direction. I pointed to the bathroom. He nodded and sat back down; scowl fixed on me as he slid the weapon into the front of his pants. A stripper cuddled to either side, caressing him. He had one hand on a girl's thigh and Tanía sat across from the trio in an old love-chair shooting beavers. In front of him, on the coffee table, lay a clear plastic bag with two fists of white powder. White lines streaked the table. A girl bent and snorted five centimeters. Then the other crazy bitch sucked up a line as long as my arm.

In the bathroom, I pissed, flushed, and sauntered back out. Tanía pointed at me. "Tomas's amigo...con Mia." Her lips were elastic, and she stuttered and yawned as she spoke. "Sientate, Cesar...este...este es, Diego."

I eased into the only empty seat, the matching beat-up love-chair across from the budding ménage. The Colombian studied my eyes, scars, arms, and muddy jeans. He clutched the closest girl and pushed her toward me. Mia noticed through the open bedroom door, jumped out, and raced across the room, bumped the girl aside, and dropped into my lap. The girl wavered there, discombobulated. Mia leaned forward and pushed her away. "No, el es mio," she snapped. I welcomed it; didn't want that nasty bitch on me, nor did I want to start trouble by dissing this Colombian.

The ill-fated creature peered through hazed-over eyes with dark shades above and below like she'd been up for days. She wore a tank-top blouse with tight dirty jeans and had flaccid breasts, arms, and legs. Her hair was grimy. She had a dark front tooth and kept wiping a leaky nose. She fell back next to the narco when Mia shoved her.

Diego was thin but sturdy with a swimmer's build. He wore three fat gold chains around his tanned neck and had black hair in a ponytail. He kept fidgeting. He'd tap the butt of the Glock in his belt, glance at me, glance at the door, do a line, and start over. He felt one bitch's tit, grabbed the other's crotch, jittered and squirmed. He reached into the bag with a pocket knife and shoveled out a pile. Tañía and the other strippers attacked it, but he watched me, not them. I didn't move; he studied that, too.

Mia didn't seem to care, though I wondered how things would've gone if Tomas and I hadn't dropped in soaking wet. She cuddled into my lap with head buried under my chin, behaving like a frightened little girl, and clung to my biceps. She didn't look at the Colombian, or the coke.

He turned to me. "Quieres un buche."

"No gracias, necesito dormir mas. Hoy llegué," I said. He twitched jaw muscles, tapped the Glock, and stared—pissed. I had to say something. So, I told him I was from Miami, a sailor, and wouldn't mind buying a kilo to take back with me on the ship. Mia's mouth dropped when I said this; I pinched her ass hard and told her to go to her room. And she obeyed . . . amazing.

Diego pretended not to be interested. He gathered his bag, and stood with white heaps left on the table. He adjusted his polo shirt over the automatic and yanked the prettier of the two strippers up by the arm. "Le hablo a Tañía mañana," he said, and dragged the aficionada to the door.

Tañía got up behind him to lock it. The other crazed bitch pressed two fingers into the pile, then shoved them into her mouth. She bowed over the table and inhaled a bunch more before the door even opened. Then she screeched, hopped up, stumbled, and squeezed by with a whirlwind of shrieks and gesticulations.

Tañía locked and latched it, then turned sleepy-eyed with a flirty grin. Mia ran out, jerked the back of my jeans, pulled me into her room, slammed the door, and started crying. What a coy, mixed-up little thing she was. Tañía stayed up snorting and sniffling until the insidious powder ran out, then slammed her door.

I slept all morning, fucked through lunchtime, ate bananas for breakfast, then went back to sleep till dark. I don't believe Tomas stirred. At dusk, Tañía wanted to call a taxi to take them to the club; I didn't let Mia go to work. And, in front of Tañía, handed her fifty dollars to go downstairs to the bodega, buy some food for us, and anything else she needed. She smothered me with kisses. Tañía gawked at the money in silence and followed Mia out the door, head bowed. I locked it and waited on the couch.

No phone, no television, not even an air conditioner. Just the furniture on a wavy floor, a scratched and dented fridge, and a rusted range with only one burner left intact. The apartment had only one slide-up window beside the door. It was secured outside with decaying steel rebar; inside it was covered with a black towel tacked to the wall with roofing nails. It still let in a breeze.

Thirty minutes later, the sisters returned carting brown-paper bags stuffed with tons of fruit, coffee, milk; a shit-load of stuff for fifty bucks. Mia even bought a bottle of Old Spice aftershave and some razors. She grinned and pointed at the three-masted schooner on the bottle like it belonged to me, or I to it.

After they packed the fridge and cabinets with the supplies, Tañía went into her room, argued with Tomas, and emerged in glaring-red jeans, a skimpy yellow top, and gaudy scarlet plastic earrings. She looked a lot like Mia, cute but chunkier, taller and cheaper-looking. She kissed her sister, thanked me, and hustled out to meet her taxi. I became conscious of my muddy jeans, bare feet, and the lack of a weapon.

Once Tañía left, I threw the sexy Mia into her bed again and banged a few hours more. Tomas slept on anesthetized and numb to the rumpus. The rest of the night revolved around gluttony, lust, and sloth: I devoured fruit, pastelitos, and tacos with cheese sauce, drank milk, then raised-the-sail again, rocked-the-boat, and passed out, sapped.

Tañía never came home. Tomas didn't care much but slummed over to the fridge in skivvies and ripped into the food.

He thanked me with guilty eyes and crumbs on his lips, burped, and dragged his dilapidated, pudgy flesh back to Tañía's bed.

Late the next morning Tañía returned. She slipped into Mia's room and lifted the sheets to look at me while I slept. Mia woke and snatched it back over us. "Que es Tañía?" she snapped. Tañía giggled with glazed eyes, and whispered that Diego sent word he'd meet with me to talk about the details and price at the club *Las Señoritas*, tonight. I gave a blank stare. She repeated Diego's name with a slur and staggered to her room.

Mia sat up, hugged her pillow and started whining. Why I was buying this if I didn't even use it? And why had I fought El Soldado? And why I had showed up here soaking wet and with no boots? I'd forgotten she'd seen everything at the club that night. She wasn't stupid. Seduced by all the sex, I told her everything about Roby, and the smuggling, and that I was going to find the chief and have him arrested for Roby's murder.

She squeezed her pillow, shook her head, and whimpered. "No, no, no...el Soldado muy peligroso, muy fuerte." I nodded and hugged her, and asked if the bodega sold clothes and shoes. She said yes. So I put my jeans on and told her to get up and go with me.

The store was owned by the Mayan woman and her husband; the one I'd seen wearing a serape in the rocking chair that first day. It also doubled as a ferreteria and had a small carniceria. And though the concrete foundation was tracked over with red mud and the ceiling fans rattled and pulsated as they pushed down the heat and scattered the constant swarm of flies, just about anything could be had down its long narrow aisles, stacked with bananas, plantains, avocados, mangos, tomatoes, yuca, malanga, boniato, papaya, guanabana, guayaba, anon, and mamey.

181

In the carniceria, there was fish and pork but no beef, pan Cubano, arroz y frijoles, and Cuban coffee; beer and liquor; American cigarettes and Hav-a-Tampa cigars. The short Mayan was in a tan guayabera with white pants tied with a thin coarse rope and leather sandals. He rarely left his counter and incessantly squinted down the aisles. He wasn't timid either. When threatened or when shouting erupted, he displayed a sawed off that looked like the one Colá had forced us over the gunwales with. If young hoodlums camped out in the aisles waiting for his head to turn, or if they gave him lip, he'd wave a machete and force them out into the streets.

The ferreteria section had coveralls and boots, gloves, sombreros and lots of tools: rakes, shovels machetes, etc. About the only things not available were drugs and women, but both could be had upstairs, or at *Las Señoritas* . . . or just about anywhere in the barrios.

I bought the biggest pair of boots (still snug), a pair of work gloves, a bunch more fruit, and trucked upstairs. I filled the sink with water, added dish soap, and dropped my jeans and t-shirt in to soak. Then I lounged on the couch in my boxers scarfing down mangos and bananas. She offered to wash the clothes and said a bar of soap was better. I didn't argue. She draped the wet stuff on the balcony to dry in the noonday sun.

As darkness approached, Tañía emerged in another bawdy outfit and said she was headed for the club again. Tomas didn't want to spend more money and slumbered on. I offered to split the cab and Mia accompanied us, dressed in faded jeans and a modest dark blouse . . . hmm? The cab traversed the hub of the barrios and anyone observing from the safety of the vehicle would have gauged the inhabitants of the muddy streets as drug dealers, addicts, putas, and thieves, but Emma Lazarus would have called them the wretched refuse yearning to breathe free. In either case, to survive here would take street savvy backed up with fists.

20:
SEÑOR DON

The taxicab sledged down the hill, fishtailed on the autopista's westbound lane slinging red mud, and spattered down to the whip-whine of a tire low on air. I sat behind the cabbie, an obese and perspiring little mulato with a gray horse-shoe balding pattern. He gnawed a cigar that couldn't suppress the odor of unwashed flesh which overpowered the tight, musty space and sticky seats. I rolled down the window. Mia held her breath; Tañía rattled down the glass on the right, panting.

I stared at the palms zipping by. Five hundred bucks left. Tomas probably had more but I couldn't count on that. Even in Venezuela, that wasn't enough to buy half a kilo, much less a whole one like Tañía had set up. Shit, what to tell Diego? Had to stall and gain his confidence.

At the mouth of the cul-de-sac, the owner of the bait shop stood with folded arms gazing toward the club. Across the street, inside the junkyard, the german shepherd charged the fence, stood on its back legs, snarled and barked. It pawed the chain link then raced back to the far side as we drove past. The neon sign that read *Las Señoritas* spotlighted the action—a fight. The cab coasted up. Tañía gasped. "Es Diego!"

Parked in front of the club, a black Mercedes idled with all four doors wide open. Two pony-tailed Colombians faced a tall, bleached-blond, shirtless, and chiselled sailor. The anchor tattooed on his bronzed arm had a long shank, a fat stock, and the crown near the elbow. As we watched, Diego rushed the sailor, and pitched a wild overhand right. The blond deflected it and clenched Diego's neck. With the other hand he grabbed the gangster's crotch, lifted him overhead, stepped forward, and launched him like a javelin head-first into the side of a dumpster. Diego stuck out an arm but his forehead thumped the rusted steel. Blood spurted, his neck twisted . . . he stayed down.

The second Colombian, taller and stockier, attacked: fists out in front and white sleeves rolled up. Once in range, he fired a quick one-two-three into the sailor's face. All landed, but only cut and stunned the goliath, who grabbed the man's ponytail with a left and smashed the Colombian's face with two right hooks. He tossed him down, then wiped his own nose with a forearm and stood there, rolling his fists like an old bare-knuckle brawler egging his opponent on. The Colombian sat on the pavement dazed and spitting blood.

The sailor was too much for them, too big, too strong. But he made a fatal mistake. He turned his back on the Don, who had sprung out from the back seat when his man went down. He yanked off his platinum jacket and whirled in white shoes and silver slacks, exposing a shoulder-holstered pistol, gold watch and bracelet. He flung the jacket inside the car and drew out a long, dark, pin-striped Louisville Slugger from the floorboards.

185

The Colombian saw his boss and leaped up. The old silver-haired Don walked quietly up behind the sailor and let go a Hank Aaron swing to the right knee. A jolting yelp echoed up the dead-end alley the way a wild boar squeals clamped in the jaws of a pit-bull. The giant crumpled; the torture began. The Don paused, bat overhead and pointing at the star-lit night with the neon backdrop; the sailor slithered away dragging a leg and holding up an arm. The next swing struck his forearm and buckled the arm—another bawl, then two bashes on the good leg. Shrieks continued.

I jumped out of the cab and marched up behind the Don, timed it, and grabbed the bat. "Ya ganó, Señor Don," I said. He squinted, released the wood, stepped aside, and clenched the butt of the pistol. I held out the bat and studied his eyes. I'd shove the handle in his mouth and smash his head in if he pulled the piece.

"Tienes guevos," he said, and seized back the handle.

From the other side of his car emerged a long-legged, dashing Latina with a butch-boy haircut, golden loops dangling from each ear, tight slacks, and a man's black, long-sleeved shirt unbuttoned to show off her milky skin. She sucked her thumb, bit a nail, caressed a breast, gawked at us, then at the unconscious, bloody Diego as the other Colombian hauled him into the back seat. The Don kicked the sailor in the balls, again in the ass, then back-stepped to the car. He drew the pistol by the rubber grip and pointed it at me, but his finger stayed outside the trigger guard. All four doors slammed, and the Mercedes peeled off. The tag—*000*.

Macho Billy Budd was a mess: splintered bone and white cartilage protruded from his bloated purple arm. The right leg dangled, half-hinged at the knee, puffed-up and twisted against his jeans. His face was gashed and pallid; he slurped and hissed quick breaths through a hacked fat lip and split, runny nose. I dragged the mangled heap to our cab. The girls jumped out. After Mia helped lay the busted fighter on the back seat, I handed the smelly driver a twenty for the ride to the hospital and told him to call another cab; I wasn't staying. He jabbered on the radio and screeched off.

The crowd gathered along the railing on the club's front deck cheered and applauded, then began chanting—"El Che, El Che." I looked at Mia, puzzled. She reached for my hand, tugged my arm, then stood on her toes and kissed my cheek.

"Che is the pueblo's redeemer," she said haltingly in English. The little faction of strippers and johns turned around, prodded each other, then shuffled and jostled through the double doors to the rhythm of a conga that spewed from the speakers.

From the middle of the cul-de-sac, standing side by side, we watched the revellers disperse into the dim club. Tañía surveyed her burgundy lips in a truck's mirror, licked two fingers, and smeared off gobs of mascara and eye shadow. Satisfied, she puckered up and imprinted a red orifice on the glass. Then turned and grinned. "Forget Diego. He's an asshole. I know some locals. You still want the kilo—right?"

"I don't know. From who?" I said.

Mia clasped my hand. "Mira el taxi." A black and yellow screeched into the alley. The driver tipped his face out the window; I waved an arm. Tañía wrenched Mia's shoulder, urged and insisted to no avail. I climbed into the back seat. Mia wrestled free and scurried to catch up. Tañía ran up to the window shouting about work and money, sailors and goodbyes, then slapped the hood, turned, and jiggled her meaty ass in glittering, green-metallic pantaloons, and never looked back. And of course, Mia played the victim: whimpered and snuggled the whole ride back.

Everybody was so wound up all the time: the girls, the shit, the barrios, the fighting. All I needed was Larosa's whereabouts. I didn't need a jonesing stripper setting up crazy deals. Her agenda was scoring to fuel her habit. But if I had some blow, maybe I could bait and chum these whores into giving up the chief. They had to know where he went, or maybe where Coño hid out. "Listen, Mia. Who'd know where El Soldado is?" The cool night air swirled through the cab; horns soared by and trailed off. "One of the girls with Diego the other night, maybe?"

"Si, si, puede ser." She nodded and cuddled. I had to think like these animals around me. What did they value? Whom did they fear? I needed leverage. If Tañía set up something small, I'd try and pull it off. The chief and his connections had to be major suppliers here. All trails would lead back to him.

The cab spattered up the hillside, past the green-tenement gang standing on the shoulder. They hunched over, peered in, and hooted seeing Mia low in my lap. She raised her head. The cab sped up to the crest and stopped in front of the bodega. I paid the driver. At least he didn't smell; a fist-sized fan hummed and vibrated on the dash.

The taxicab spun away and the old Mayan woman came into view rocking in her chair. She waved as if she'd known me for years. Her husband beckoned through the big window scribed in the white lettering. We nodded back and trudged by into the trash-can-alley that led to the rooms.

At the foot of the stairs, a Dominican haggled with a girl in pyjamas leaning on the handrail. Cats scrambled from our path and disappeared into shadows. A white one leaped out of the dumpster. When the couple saw us, he took money; she snatched something from his other hand, wheeled, and bolted up the steps. He ducked and hurried to the roadway. The girl dashed into room 6, slammed the door, and rattled it secure. Mia turned to me. "Esta loca." She was our neighbor—the battered one.

Inside, Tomas had the refrigerator wide open and hovered in skivvies, pigging out. He turned around, scratched his balls, then wiped salsa-smeared lips and flashed buck teeth. "Hope you're buying next time," I said. He nodded, shoved in another tamale, chewed, swallowed, chugged the milk and tossed the carton in the trash. Mia locked the door, raced to her room, and plopped face first on the Olive Oyl pillowcase. I dropped onto the couch.

Tomas trotted to Tañía's room. When he returned, he handed over fifty bolivares and said "Gracias, Gracias, Gracias."

Mia stopped snivelling and came back out. She meekly squeezed in on the couch and spooned her round little cheeks into my cock. I draped an arm over her and dropped Tomas's money in her lap. "Go buy some tacos and fajitas, or whatever you want." She didn't move. But after fifteen minutes of silence, she gathered the bills and stomped out.

Tomas materialized from his cave in new work pants and a snug white t-shirt with a roll of hairy fat popping out over the unbuttoned pants. He plunked into a chair and blinked at me. "So . . . what have you found out?"

"Not much. He's not in La Guaira. That's about all."

"So now what?"

"Your girl, Tañía, says she knows some locals who used to work with him, moving shit on the cargo ships."

"So, she's going to ask them where he's at?"

"No, she's setting up a score, and I'll ask them."

"Whatever. They won't tell you mierda, For this we jumped ship?"

"Well, that's my only lead." He grinned. I lay silent on my side and stared a long while. Then kicks banged the door and Mia screeched my name. I sat up slowly and rubbed my face. She kicked harder and screamed. "Yes, yes…I'm coming," I yelled.

When I opened the door, she rushed by and spilled a grocery bag. Behind her stood a creepy thin teenager with an afro, silver-piercing through his lips and ears, a tie-dyed shirt, ripped jeans, and holes in his sneakers. He began ranting and mumbling. I didn't say a word and plastered a right-cross into the heart of his gibberish. The tall, skinny bastard flipped over the railing and landed in a hibiscus bush. I thought he was dead. But he squirmed free and crawled out, crying and cussing. He waddled about on hands and knees searching for rocks to throw and settled for a mud-ball. The throw was so awkward and weak, I batted it down and he hobbled off, holding his back with one hand and feeling the busted lip with the other—poor freaked-out kid.

After Tomas and Mia put away the food she leaped into my arms, whining. "I don't want to live here anymore. I want to go to Miami with you."

I just hugged her. Tomas rolled his eyes and went to his room. I lifted Mia up and into bed then pounded and slapped that tight little ass for a long while. Tomas hammered the wall to Mia's blissful hysteria. I didn't care. The best remedy for a girl crying in your arms is a rough lay. That postpones any crisis for at least a day.

Around eleven Tañía returned all keyed up. She blabbed on about three locals from Barquisimeto who'd showed up at the club. She'd convinced them to sell me an ounce of clean shit straight off an aparato from Colombia. That was what they called a brick, or a kilo. She added that I'd get it cheaper with dollars instead of bolivares. I said I'd think about it. She bragged, "They do business with El Soldado." That convinced me, but I felt led on and decided to take Tomas along.

The instructions: meet at half past midnight, at the west end of the port, where the fence line met the water's edge away from the autopista, and less than a mile from the strip club. Tomas said he knew the spot, and agreed to be backup . . . and that three hundred US would be enough. So we left the girls and hustled down the stairs.

***

It was already 2330 hours. The taxi showed up after twenty minutes. The driver was Mr. Horseshoe Swine again, and I was tempted to complain but let it go. Tomas coughed and sniffed loudly then stuck his head out the window as we came to a stop.

Blue lights flickered a mile down the hill. The cab slowed to a crawl. Ten more minutes passed as we inched by the green tenement where four policia patrols had swarmed the gang outside. Three lay cuffed on their stomachs with faces in the mud. A cop in black riot gear stood over them pointing a rifle at their heads.

We reached the autopista at quarter past, and I told Pigsty to punch it. He dropped us on the sidewalk at twenty five after, on his watch; Roby's busted one was in my pocket—I never left it behind.

191

We jogged along the fence line toward the ocean. I hadn't seen it in almost a week, and still didn't. The dark sea reflected the city lights. From the corner, where the fence reached the edge of the wall, the channel led east to the port. The running lights of a ship were moving out from the mouth of the harbor. Along the west side, out to sea, the levee had park benches with tall royal palms situated for sightseers to sit under and watch the ships churn through. Waves splashed. In the parking lot a bright yellow convertible honked. Two mulato guys and a mestizo jumped over the doors and marched at us. Tomas elbowed me. "That's them."

My heartbeat accelerated. The corner was dark and there was only one escape—back along the fence to the autopista. All three wore white tank-tops and blue jeans. Their arms had gang tattoos. They formed a line and headed in long strides toward us. Hard gazes darted from Tomas to me and back. Their pace quickened. The center one started jogging. Once in earshot he yelled out, "Tienes dollares o bolivares?"

"Dollares," Tomas answered. Instantly, one mulato yanked out a wooden, hand-sized, Aztec-decorated bat from behind his back and bolted at him. The other two rushed at me, silent and vicious.

I filled my lungs, grunted like a linebacker, ducked and tackled the closest one. I landed on his scrawny frame and smashed a right and left into his face before the mestizo bulled into me. I landed on rocky ground with him on my side. A white flash and his fist busted my nose. A second punch glanced off my forehead. I spun and maneuvered to side control. When I braced on the ground, my hand gripped a cold, heavy stone. I beat the son-of-a-bitch senseless. Blood sprayed every time I connected.

192

I turned to see Tomas and the third guy rolling on the ground. Still holding the bloody stone, I sprinted over and clubbed that bastard out. Tomas stood and kicked him in the face. Then the first guy came around. I ran back and punched him in the solar plexus. He lay gasping for air; the others were unconscious.

While he lay there filling his lungs, I stood over him and yelled like a raging psychopath. "Do you know El Soldado Larosa? Where is he? Do you know the Mexican, Coño?" He shot a bird at me as he wheezed and huffed. So, still raging, and to Tomas's wide open eyes, I lifted the unconscious mestizo on my shoulder, carried him to the edge of the pier, told the other bastard to watch, and threw his buddy into the channel. He sank.

The mulato crawled to the edge but I kicked his ribs and ranted my questions again. He punched my thigh and tried to jump in after his friend. I pulled him back by his spiked hair and punched his ribs again. I yanked his head up and spat into his bloody face. "Tell me. And you better hurry."

"El Soldado esta en Puerto Cabello," he grunted out. Then he staggered to his feet and asked if the chief owed me money before he dove in after his friend. The other son-of-a-bitch never came round. Tomas and I galloped to the autopista, ran, and ran.

21:
THE PIT

We sprinted until Tomas's lungs and legs gave out. He bent over and coughed. A bus whooshed by. I braced against the perimeter fence that secured the pier and warehouses, filled my lungs, and chucked out a bloody wad. "I hope that bastard drowns." I wiped blood off my nose and hacked again. "And I'm gonna bitch-slap that junky stripper of yours—Tañía. Those bastards would've killed us."

"Casi-casi." Tomas peered at me from behind a puffed-up eyelid, scraped and welted forehead, and raised a bruised, distended forearm like a gladiator. I snorted out more blood, wiggled the loose tingling cartilage of my nose, wheezed, and leaped into a vigorous stride. Tomas struggled to keep up, dangling the battered arm, so I eased up, but still kept a good pace.

We couldn't stop, call, and wait for a taxi. Not after that scene, and two possible deaths. We stayed on the sidewalk and jogged along the fence line. Traffic was sparse. After some headway, we scouted the autopista in hopes of an empty cab. Halogen light-posts showered the desolate highway with a sallow glow. The streets were empty except for the carcass of a dog, splattered and scattered across the center line. It was late; we pushed on, checking behind us now and again.

After a mile, maybe two, the road split and the chain link angled toward the docks. We followed the eastbound sidewalk, which was lined with fenced scrap yards, boatyards, and marine mechanic shops. Side streets led to more hillside neighborhoods with tenement flats along the toe of the slope.

Not long after we'd given up hope, a red and white taxi cruised up and honked. We scrambled aboard. The driver studied us through the cage that separated us from him. Satisfied, he slapped the meter's arm, and sped off.

In front of the bodega, I rolled out. Tomas flung bolivares at the cabbie. I charged, gung ho, into the alley toward the stairs, clenched the handrail, and leaped two steps with each stride. I marched to the end, balled and squeezed my right hand, and hammer-fisted door 7. Tomas braced on the railing and huffed up the stairs.

The latch slid, the chain rattled, and Tañía yanked the door open, giggling. She gasped at my wild eyes and busted nose. Hollering "Puta," I clutched her throat, plowed in two steps, and shoved her toward the couch. Mia and two other girls screamed as Tañía fell over the coffee table and landed on the next-door neighbor's lap. I grabbed one end of the table and flipped it across the room, scattering the tray of razor blades and straws. "Those bastards tried to rob us, and would've killed us—stupid!" Four pairs of wide eyes gawked up; Mia covered her wide-open mouth. Tomas shuffled in and latched the door. I pointed. "His arm is broken. Is there a clinic near by?"

"No, no estoy bien," he said and toddled to the kitchen sink. Groans accompanied the splatter of running water. Mia followed him and returned with a wet paper towel and bottle of peroxide.

But I couldn't stand still and paced, pumped like Jake LaMotta waiting for the bell. I kicked the chairs and punched the walls. The crazy neighbor clasped her girlfriend's hand and dashed for the door. I blocked their escape. The two stood paralyzed as I leaned against the door. "No one's leaving. Tañía, do those gang-bangers know where you live?"

"No, but they can go to the club and ask."

"Tomas, we've got to go." His grumbling continued from the kitchen. "Sit down, girls. You're not leaving." The Latinas cowered away and squeezed back on the couch holding hands.

"Well, you wanted to buy perico," Tañía jeered.

"You said they were friends."

"Go fuck seagulls if you can't handle it."

"Can't handle it? I busted down those low-life criminals— ask Tomas. And you know what else—stupid bitch. No matter how low you go, or how holy you think you are, there's still a right and a wrong. And those thugs crossed the line."

She put a hand over her eyes and mocked me with a whimper, then joined her friends on the couch. Mia rinsed the gash on my nose with peroxide, pressed the paper into the cut to stop the bleeding, then went for ice. I glared at Tañía. "And why are these girls here?"

"They wanted to party." She smirked, and kissed the crazy neighbor from room 6. Mia came back with ice cubes wrapped in a wash rag and stood beside me checking my new cuts and old scars. The ice burned. I paced and schemed; she rearranged the coffee table and took a chair. Her brown eyes followed my movements like a timekeeper losing time.

Tomas sauntered in carrying a towel loaded with ice cubes and plopped into a love chair. He didn't glance at Tañía. She stayed on the couch with the aficionadas and ogled his now-blackened arm, welted forehead, and closed eye. I paced; they watched: back and forth, back and forth.

"Tomas, you think it's broken?"

"Crushed and splintered maybe, but not broken," he muttered. Tañía lowered her eyes.

"So we can leave?" I said. He nodded. Mia's jaw flopped open. "Then we go at dawn before those bastards get some friends and come looking for us." She stomped to her room. I glared at the nut from next door and her friend. "And what are your names?"

"Lola, y mi amiga, Zulu." She fluttered eyelids and smiled. They both wore shorts, one red the other orange, and white tank-top blouses with hard nipples peeking through. Both were attractive but scrawny and beat up. Lola had one grayish eye and the other light blue, pockmarks on her cheeks, and stiff brown hair. Zulu's nose was thin and brittle as if the cartilage was missing. A knife had scarred one side of her neck and she never talked.

I ranted on. Something in my pocket pricked my skin. I pulled out Roby's watch: the crystal was shattered and both hands were bent. I shoved it back in my pocket.

I needed a weapon: gun, bat, machete . . . anything. Maybe we could take a bus to Puerto Cabello . . . or a taxi? Can't let the girls know where I'm going. What if those thugs hunt for us tonight? No, it's too late. They're in the hospital. Besides, the club's closed now and won't open until lunch. We have some time—hours . . . a few hours.

I spent those hours before dawn peeking around the black towel that covered the window, checking Tomas's arm, and keeping the bored and horny girls at bay. The vague image of the chief throwing Roby overboard fuelled my anger. The promise I'd made to Mom kept me focused, plotting.

Tañía crawled off to bed. Tomas dozed in the chair until the ice soaked the armrest. The lesbian lovers stretched out on the couch, embraced. Mia locked her bedroom door, and I paced.

As the morning hue slipped around the black curtain, someone knocked next door. I pressed an ear against ours. The banging continued on the adjacent door. "Lola, Lola . . . es Mario," the man shouted.

Lola sat up, rubbed her eyes, and gaped around, bewildered. Mario must be one of her steady johns. He kept pounding, so I let her out. They kissed and went inside her place. Zulu snored.

I secured the front door, woke Tomas, and knocked on Mia's. She opened it stark naked, wiping tears from her cheeks. Her skin glistened in the faint light. She was a temptress with her shaved muff and muscular body. But I was paranoid; dying was on my mind, not sex. I kissed and hugged her, wiped away her tears and kissed her puffy eyes. Then said I had to leave. That one day I'd come back for her. She forced a smile, turned and jumped on her bed into the Popeye-pillow, sniveling.

Tomas wobbled to the kitchen, wolfed down some pastelitos, and chugged orange juice from a carton. I inhaled a banana, and we emerged from our sanctuary into the hazy light.

We paused outside. I leaned over the railing and studied the alley, then the passageway to the roadway—all quiet and vacant. Cats stalked the dumpster; crows cawed, perched on the edge, and bounced in and out with scraps in their beaks. Nothing new.

198

So we edged down the steps and into the trash-can alley, swivel-necked. It was just after seven and the elderly Mayan battled the mud on the front porch with a worn-out broom. Draped in her multicolor wool serape, the old woman shoveled scraps onto a tray for the herd of cats. The couple gazed at our injuries and simply nodded. Tomas called for a cab; I kept sentry.

Even out here, the taxis never took longer than fifteen or twenty minutes to show up but after forty minutes—still nothing. We plunked down on the porch. At eight, the bodega's first patron staggered up in flip-flops and dirty gray work clothes. He stumbled inside. After bickering with the old Indian, he returned sipping on a half-pint of dark liquor and drifted past us to some unknown burrow in the muddy alley.

Something wasn't right. I was pondering buying one of the machetes I'd seen in the tool section when a red and white taxi pulled up the hill and stopped. Tomas climbed in. I hesitated but decided that we could stop and buy one later.

First thing that struck me was the cage. I recognized it. And the driver…was he the same guy who'd driven us home last night? I'd never taken a good look. I'd been too pissed. But yes . . . could be. Then Tomas asked, "I called the yellow cab, didn't I?"

The cabbie said he'd heard the dispatch over the radio and happened to be nearby. I didn't believe him but then again— why not?

I asked if he'd take us to Puerto Cabello at a flat rate. He complained that it was seventy-five kilometers away and he'd have to call in. He added that the bus was cheaper and slugged down the hill toward the autopista.

Finally leaving the barrio, I felt relieved. Puerto Cabello was west of La Guaira so the route on the autopista went past the club and the docks. As we reached the highway, he squawked on the radio then spun his head around and said no. We'd have to get a different cab, or he could take us to the bus station. I said the bus. As we approached the cul-de-sac to the club, Tomas and I slumped down in the back seat, just in case.

The automatic door locks clicked down and the cab whipped into the dead end. I sprang up and punched the cage, "Cabron! What the fuck are you doing?"

Parked in front of the club was the yellow convertible, along with a black Chevy Crew-Cab Dually. "Son of a bitch!" I lay flat on the back seat and kicked my window. I was frantic; the cab was locked. The first kick spider-webbed it; the second sent a slab of glass flying out and scattered fragments over me and the seat. The driver slammed on the brakes. I bounced onto the floorboard with a boot sticking through the window. Tomas's forehead bashed off the cage. Now we were stuck . . . like crabs in a box trap.

I struggled to sit upright. Two Colombians and the mulato I'd fought on the docks came up to my side. I squirmed over Tomas and tried his door. Locked. Another mulato brandished a galvanized pipe, smiling in at me through the window. His head was partially shaved and bandaged.

Then the locks clicked up and the yelling started. "Salgan del carro!" A Colombian reached in, seized Tomas by the hair, and yanked him out. The mulato opened the other door and swung the pipe. I blocked it with a boot. The other Colombian crawled in behind me and punched the top of my head. I grabbed his hair; he clutched my arm. We rolled and grappled.

Heavy steel walloped my thigh; my leg buzzed numb. They dragged me out by the dead foot as I punched and kicked.

On the glass-covered pavement, we sat with our backs against the cab's running board. I could see the mestizo in the back seat of the convertible; his head wrapped in white bandage. He hadn't drowned after all. The two mulatos and the two Colombians stood over us carrying bats and pipes. Suddenly the passenger side of the truck opened and out popped the Don. The autopista was two hundred yards away and we were on the blind side of the cab. No one else could see; they'd set it up well.

The silver haired Don marched over. No fancy suit this time. He was in cowboy boots, jeans, and a brown leather coat. He seemed taken back when he saw me. "Segunda vez que nos encontramos," he muttered. I gaped, unable to speak.

He said, "Your business with these gangsters is not my concern. They tried to rob you—right?"

"Si, Señor Don."

"They have no honor. But you've learned respect somewhere," he said.

I nodded. Tomas gawked. The Colombians hovered over us. One kept his hand on a Glock in his belt; the other rolled a bat. Each mulato had a pipe. The Don nodded at his bodyguards and told the mulatos they could leave, then turned to me again. "My only concern here is why you asked about El Soldado. Why do you look for him? How do you know this man?" The sports car idled away.

What could I say? That I wanted to kill the son of a bitch? That the chief owed me money? Whatever I said, I couldn't give it up too easily, or he'd know I was lying. So I stared at him— silent. Tomas stared at the pavement holding his battered arm. All the while, the cabby waited, bobbing his head to merengue.

The Don pulled out a black comb from his jean pocket and slicked back his lengthy hair. "Is this about money? Or something else?"

I still said nothing. He smiled and handed the cabby a roll of cash and told him to leave. The bodyguards stood us up and shoved us toward the truck. One pointed his Glock, while the second duct-taped our hands behind our backs. Tomas started sniveling and I had to tighten my butt-cheeks to keep from shitting my pants.

They pushed and heaved us into the back seat. The Don climbed in front. One bodyguard slid in next to Tomas. The other jumped in and started the truck. The diesel rattled. The Don kicked on the air conditioner. "It's going to be a hot morning." He turned around in the seat to look at us. "Still nothing to say?"

"The chief owes me money," I said. "I want to find him and get paid. It's business."

"So it's business. But how do you know him?"

"I'm a sailor from Miami. I worked on the cargo ship with him. I gave him money for half a brick and he left without giving it to me."

"Miami. Half a brick. Hmm . . . no se si te creo. Ignacio, let's take them for a ride." The truck thundered down the dead-end lane and made a left. The Don frowned at Tomas. "And you? What's your story?"

"He just knows the girls where we stayed," I said. The Don glared at me. The bodyguard in the back seat leaned across Tomas's lap and punched my mouth. My head jerked back and bounced off the side-window. Blood dripped from my lip onto the carpeting.

The Don looked at Tomas again. "I was saying . . . what's your story?"

"Yo soy . . . marinero también. Y conozco a Tañía—y la hermana." Tomas quivered.

The Don turned front and faced the road. The truck curved off the autopista and onto a two lane mountain road and powered up the hillside. He put on the radio—classical music. Mozart or Beethoven, I didn't know. I didn't give a shit. I was sweating despite the wide-open air conditioner. What a stupid way to end. I thought of Roby and my parents. Blood dripped down my chin. I twisted my wrist to gnaw at the tape. It was wrapped too tight and too thick. Tomas leaned forward and rested his forehead against the back of the seat. He looked over at me; his eyes watered. I clenched my jaw and hissed short breaths. Blood trickled onto my shirt. How could I beat these guys? The truck roared on.

The Don peeked back at me. "This young Cubanito from Miami has balls. Lots of cuts too. You a fighter? What's your name?" I didn't answer. My lungs felt collapsed. I just glared at him, and sucked air. "OK . . . I'll call you Cubanito." He nodded at me and turned back around.

After a long while of nothing but farmhouses or mountainside jungle, we bounced off the main road onto a cleared range. The truck stopped and the driver, Ignacio, jumped out. He locked the hubs on the front wheels, climbed back in, and stuck the rig in four-wheel drive. We spun to the end of the clearing and stopped next to a track-hoe the size of a gantry-crane. He put the Chevy in park and left it idling.

One bodyguard hauled Tomas out; the other came for me. He didn't touch me. He just pulled his Glock and gestured me out. I obeyed. I thought of Mom and Dad . . . and Roby. My knees weakened. They turned us around with stomachs against the truck and wrapped duct tape over our eyes. "What have I done to you guys?" I yelled.

The Don's calm voice again, "Why do you look for the chief?"

"I told you. The son of a bitch gave me his word and kept my money." I was desperate. "What about honor?"

No reply. They pushed us along. Tomas whimpered. I could tell his nose was congested. I could barely walk. A shove, a second one, and I dropped.

I plummeted onto a hairy balloon; it popped. Putrid hot slime shot up from under my boots, splattered up my chest and hit my chin. I toppled forward and landed face first on a hairy sack of bones . . . like a burlap sack but denser. Flies swarmed my shaved head; little legs skipped across my face. Some crawled into my nose. I snorted and shrieked.

I heard Tomas screaming, too, then the Don's voice again from somewhere above us. "I'll see El Soldado very soon. I'll ask him about you. You are not my enemy. I have no reason to end your life. But I advise you to leave Venezuela. This is your lucky day, Cubanito. But so you don't forget."

Automatic fire crackled. Pops and clicks filled my ears. Hot sap splattered through the air like warm rain. I balled up in the fetal position while droplets and bits showered me in baptism. The firing continued for almost a minute. It sounded like water balloons popping. The same sound a wave makes when it plops into a pocket of a stone, only louder and repetitive. Sometimes a burst and a discharge of gas as if a tire blew out.

Then silence, followed by slamming doors . . . and the fading rumble of the truck's engine.

"Tomas! Tomas!"

"Si . . . si," he whined. The stench was overwhelming. The air was rancid with the smell of rotting meat. I choked; my stomach turned. I vomited and heard Tomas doing the same. My pants . . . I had shit my pants. My eyes filled with tears. I rolled on the squalid, hairy carcasses until the tape over my eyes snagged a splintered bone. I twisted my neck to rip it away.

We were in a square pit of rotting animals: two horses, a goat and a calf hacked up like hamburger. I gagged and retched again. The sun was already hot. The flies clouded the air in black. Maggots swarmed over the raw meat like a filthy locust horde.

The edge of the pit was eight or nine feet up. About as high as the basketball hoop Roby and I had cemented in Mom's driveway. I rolled over to Tomas and gripped the tape over his eyes with my teeth. My partial shifted and started to come out. I used my chin. He wedged his head into mine and we rolled the tape off one eye. He rubbed off the other side against my shoulder.

We squirmed like caterpillars in cocoons to a spot without a dead animal. The flies buzzed over us, on us, sometimes in us: mouth, nose, eyes and ears. If I concentrated, I could hear the swishing-swooshing of a million maggots feeding. We retched and choked again. Crazed, Tomas jumped to his feet and started running in a circle. He tripped, rolled onto the hacked-up calf, and started ranting, "We're gonna die. The bulldozers will cover us with dirt. We're gonna die."

"Good. Keep yelling. Someone will hear and help us," I said. Tomas raved on. The fly-cloud lifted and nestled back to feast and fester.

At noon, there was no place to hide from the burning sun. From certain angles, I could see a wave of decomposing gases mixed with flies rising from our tomb. I was spinning and Tomas was flighty. Hands still taped, I wobbled on my knees to one of the horse carcasses. The flesh was decomposing so the rib cage protruded. I kicked the slimy ribs until one snapped, then turned and fell back onto the carcass. I shoved my taped hands into its soupy gut and gripped the busted bone, pushed and pulled until it split and snapped free.

Back to Tomas, I crawled on my knees. "Take it and hold it firm. I'll saw the tape against it." After several prompts, he clasped it, and I began rubbing my wrist against the serrated bone. I spat flies out and sawed back and forth until one side gave. I twisted my wrist and ripped the last few strands, then stood, lifting my fists. "I'm still alive . . . you bastards."

My hands trembled as I cut Tomas loose. Every few minutes, the flies would settle on our faces and we would scrub them off, screaming. Moments later, we'd do it again; they were driving us into hysteria. "Hurry, get on my shoulders." I cupped my hands. Tomas put in a boot and leaned on the muddy wall. I lifted and he placed a boot on my shoulder and stretched out an arm.

His elbows reached the edge. "There's nothing to grab," he yelled.

The bastard was heavy and I was weak. My weight shifted, a knee buckled, and he crashed onto my shoulder. We lay on top of each other covered in animal parts and noxious oily slime. We caught a breath, tried again, and tumbled again.

A huge, rancid, decaying stew—that's what we were in. Worse than a cargo hold full of fertilizer, and we couldn't reach topside. I lost hope. I sweltered in the heat and foul air, and watched the moving carpet of maggots consume the dead. I stopped swatting flies and let them cover me.

Hours passed, then came the rumble of an engine. Them again? No way. No way. Then came beeping. A vehicle backed up to the edge—a dump truck. The bed lifted and down slid a dead cow. We stood pressed against a side and closed our eyes. It slapped on top of the horse carcass ejecting guts in all directions. Tomas began screaming, "Ayuda! Ayuda!"

I joined in. "Help us. Help!"

An old farmer in jean overalls and a straw hat stretched over the edge. He began yapping about what the hell we were doing inside his disease-pit. He tossed down a chain. Tomas gripped high; I clutched a link low and wrapped my wrist. The chain squeezed tight and the truck hoisted us as we dragged against the mud wall.

Topside, the old man gave us some rags to clean up with. We lay in the searing bed of his truck, silent, and gawked at the ocean-blue sky as he drove back to town.

22:
PUERTO CABELLO

We lay stretched out in the bed of the truck. Heads banged on the hot steel. Eyes glanced at treetops and blue sky. I sat up against the back of the cab. The sides were 2x6's made into a rail fence and shoved into the post-slots in the lift-bed. The mountain shrank behind us, framed between the side-boards.

Once you've set out to do violence, you must accept that violence can be done to you. I understood what those words meant, but it's another thing to be on the short end of that statement. I felt castrated, humbled. We'd been lucky. And soon the chief would know I hunted him. How soon? And who was I to hunt down a soldier? Thugs were getting the best of me.

When we reached the highway, the farmer turned into a service station—Valero. I jumped out and ran to the rest room. Inside I took off my boots and pants and rinsed out my skid-stained briefs. Then I filled a sink, cupped both hands, scooped and splashed water all over myself. I jumped about naked, scrubbing, and left a puddle on the grungy tile. Tomas walked in mumbling to himself and rubbing his eyes. He took over the sink and stood for a moment, staring into the mirror. He wouldn't talk to me and ducked his head when I looked his way. When I flushed the urinal, he flinched at the blast from the water pressure and continued staring into the mirror and dousing his face with water.

The station was on the outskirts of town and at the edge of the farmlands. Inside, I bought a Coca Cola and a few overripe bananas. The store catered to farmers and had a hardware section, like the Mayan bodega. I bought a machete and slid my belt through the loop of the sheath so it would hang. It had a wooden handle and sharp blade. It was much heavier than the commercial brands I'd seen in the States. I practiced a swing and a thrust, tensed my neck, filled my veins with blood, and gritted my teeth, thinking of the bullets flying. I'd been tossed into battle, bruised and beaten, but I was still in pursuit of the justice due me. Mine was a noble cause, a reckoning. God had watched over us . . . or was it a warning? My hand trembled. I pictured the cow splattering over the horse carcass. Tears filled my eyes. The pops of gunfire haunted my ears . . . the maggots swish-swashing through the rotting meat. The flies . . . the smell.

The flat-bed cranked up and the farmer honked. I rushed to his window. "Would you drive us to Puerto Cabello? I'll pay."

The old Venezuelan removed the straw hat, scratched a bald head, and dragged a bandana across the beads of sweat on his tanned brow. "En otro camion," he said. So Tomas and I climbed back onto the flat-bed, and he drove to his ranch house to switch trucks.

He made a u-turn, drove about a mile, and rumbled up a driveway to an aging hacienda we'd passed along the way. I'd read in some Defoe novel how the Spanish and Portuguese colonials had built their homes on the hillsides to defend against pirates. This place had seen its share of windstorms. The decaying pillars on the wraparound porch that supported the tile roof were built of stone and mortar. In a mowed field his grandchildren played futbal.

Tomas and I sat in the bed and watched the children play. Three brothers. All three were about the same height. And all were kicking the ball at the same time, pushing and tugging at each other. A passenger van cranked up and the farmer pulled up next to the flat-bed. Tomas climbed into the back seat and stretched out. I jumped in the front, and we were off.

He was a friendly old coot: tanned face, white dentures, and bulgy veins on calloused hands. He stopped at the end of the driveway and turned to me. "Cuanto tienes?" He spoke Castilian Spanish—quite proper for a guajiro. We bartered for a moment and agreed on a hundred dollars, which left me with a hundred and change. Seventy-five kilometres is less than fifty miles. So a dollar a mile was fair. I gave him the hundred dollar bill; he raised an eyebrow. "Are you going to the festival in Puerto Cabello—Día de la Raza?"

"Si, soy marinero," I said.

"Do you know where Puerto Cabello gets its name?"

"No. But cabello means hair."

"The harbor is so smooth sailors said giant vessels could be made fast to the docks with a single strand of hair." He chuckled and kept talking. I pretended to listen, but my thoughts drifted to my present fix. The sun was half way to the horizon and darkness was not far behind. What would I do once I got there? I sifted through dozens of scenarios.

The hour long trip passed like minutes. Tomas never moved and stared at the rusty metal roof the entire ride. The farmer stopped on a hillside roadway. He pointed at the sparkling port a mile below. Tomas sat up in the back seat. I jumped out and walked around to the driver side and shook the farmer's hand. "Gracias. It is good to find an honorable man."

He glanced at the machete in my belt. "Vaya con Dios, joven."

Tomas told him not to leave yet, shuffled out, and stood before me. "I'm not staying, Cesar. I've kept my word. I'm going home to Maracaibo." My mouth dropped; was I alone again? He continued. "You are a guerrero, Cesar. And perhaps Dios is watching over you. But for me the pit was an omen. If I go with you, I will die. I love my wife and my children. I go to be with them now."

He gave me an abrazo on one side and then the other. "You and I are like soldiers now—brothers from battles . . . and sailors first. Goodbye Cesar—vaya con Dios." He jumped in the front seat and told the farmer to take him to the ferrocarril— train station. He hung his head out the window, reached out and clasped my hand.

"Yes, we're hermanos now, Tomas," I said.

"We are, Cesar. I leave you to your destiny—your choice. But as a brother, I will tell you one last thing. Go get Mia. Save her from these barrios. She loves you. Forget the savage you've become. Forget this deed of yours. Pursuing vengeance will destroy you."

"We are truly brothers, Tomas. I shall not forget you." Maybe they were wise words, but I had a promise to keep. I squeezed his hand until the torque of the van ripped loose my grip. It sputtered off. I've never felt so alone—helpless. I hadn't anticipated this. Hell, I couldn't remember the last thing I'd done right. But in the end, I could only count on myself, my drive, my spirit—my wrath.

I could hear music rising up from the port. On the gentle slope behind me was a flourishing banana plantation. I was hungry. I wandered through the shady stocks with ripe racimos hanging in abundance. I slid out the machete, pictured the chief's neck, and sliced a thick watery shoot with one wild stroke. Sticky sap splattered my face; the eight-foot stock crashed down. I gorged.

I waited until dusk; didn't want to stand out in the crowd. No more mistakes. No more. Surprise was my only advantage. But where would I look for him? An apple never falls far from the tree. Whores go to whorehouses. The chief was a whore because he acted out of greed to protect his corrupt world. He had no principles. He'd killed my brother, his captain's son, his shipmate who'd trusted him.

I sprang up, drew the machete and thrust the point into a shoot, then another, sliced a third, and another, again and again, grunting and screaming. The stalks tumbled like masts struck by a cannonball. The clump remained with only knee-high stalks. I dropped to my knees, wept and wept. Jumped up again, and hollered, "Bastard," and destroyed a second clump of banana stocks. The machete fit my grip.

I had to conquer my fears. I practiced shoving and forcing the machete deep into the fleshy stocks. The chief would bleed red just like anyone else. He was a mortal man of flesh and blood. I would walk in the shadows until I found him. I'd be the shadow. I had left my persona—an athlete, a student, a philosopher no more. I'd breathe the air of bears. I'd be a ghost and float on the wind. I'd rip him and shred him like the tigers at the whale carcass. Could I do it? Could I kill him? Lord help me. Why would God help me break his own commandment? A mosquito landed on my face. I slapped it, and started scrubbing and swatting away the flies again . . . but there were no flies. I bawled, cleaned my eyes, jumped up screaming and attacked a third clump, and shredded the stocks, and stabbed it over and over with wild frantic swings. The cambium layers hung like strands of white hair.

When does a good man decide to be a killer? To protect his life, his family? But Roby was already dead. Was I the avenging angel? Was that what Tomas had meant?—that Dios protects me? Was I still on the side of right? To chop off the head of a snake is easy. But a man's? Would I even get that close? Soldiers shoot from far away; assassins creep close. I wept 'til I had strength to cry no more, then squatted among the fallen stocks for a long while wondering what next to do.

The sun disappeared and left a crimson line on the horizon. I got up off my knees, wiped my eyes, glared up at the fading light and shouted. "Don't let me die, Lord! Let me avenge my innocent brother." I cleaned the machete on my jeans; smeared mud over the blood stains on my shirt, slapped my face until it hurt, and started down the road to the festival.

***

Puerto Cabello was larger than Puerto La Guaira. The festival was being held along the oceanside esplanade. Tents set up facing the channel were selling arepas, torta de joyotto, tamales, pasteles and lots of fruit. Others had kegs of beer and party bowls filled with sangria. Tons of people everywhere, dancing erotically in tangas and tiny bikinis; couples rubbed half-naked sweaty bodies together in heated displays. On a central stage, musicians played Joropo rhythms with improvised vocals. The band had four string guitars, trumpets, marcas, bongos, and

213

even a harp. Hundreds of couples danced. Girls jiggled in grass-like skirts with tangas underneath. Men dressed like African deities with colorful Indian feathers. Some wore painted animal masks of lions, tigers, and leopards along with the skins draped over them like serapes.

I learned that the festival commemorated the arrival of Christopher Columbus, but Día de la Raza meant Day of Indigenous Resistance . . . that accounted for the wild African milieu. The beat of the music, and the alcohol, pumped me full of courage and vainglory. I scrutinized anyone who resembled the chief mate. I staggered through the crowd with the machete hanging from my belt, in a filthy t-shirt and mud-wiped jeans.

In the first hour, I hiked from one end of the festival to the other at least ten times, and stopped at the punch bowl for sangria at the onset of every lap. From one end of the port, I could see the massive towers of the San Felipe Fortress guarding the entrance to the channel. On the opposite side stood a cathedral built of Spanish stone and stained glass windows. The music played on; one band would quit and another would take the stage.

I marched back and forth between the fortress and the cathedral all night. By midnight I was drunk. I stumbled around talking to myself about: the chief, Coño, his brothers, Roby, the Colombians, the pit, Tañia, Tomas, little Mia, and the green-eyed sorority sister, my boxing coach, my father—the shiny navy captain . . . and Mom…and my promise—my purpose. Finally, I gave up looking for Larosa at the festival and lurched down the main avenue, aimlessly crossing streets and zigzagging through the pueblo. I slipped into a side-street with a row of brothels.

Unlike *Las Señoritas* in La Guaira, these cantinas had prostitutes standing outside selling pussy. The bouncers were their pimps. Red lamps marked the doorways but the street was dark except for light posts at the corners. Inside the first dive, two men played pool at a corner table shrouded in cigarette smoke. My eyesight was blurred. They stared at me; I stopped, studied their faces until they dropped their eyes, then strolled to the bar. The bartender was burly, a pudgy-faced asshole with a wart on his chin and wide open eyes. "Conoces un marinero que le dicen El Soldado Larosa?" I asked him.

He shook his head. "Quieres tomar?"

"Si dame tequila," I muttered. He brought out a bottle with a worm in it, like in Mexico. He poured a shot and put a wedge of lime on the counter. I threw it back, slammed down the shot-glass, and bit the lime. Fuck, that was nasty. I paid and wobbled out.

The next cantina had several girls outside; I bumped into the prettiest one and grabbed her ass. She turned. "Fucky-fucky—fifty dollars. Sucky-sucky—twenty."

I smiled. She'd made me for an American right away. "Conocen El Soldado?"

"No. Fucky-fucky," she insisted. I walked inside. The place was empty. I did another shot and back to the street.

After eight or nine cantinas, I was lost. My head was spinning.

The next bar had a box playing a reggae beat. This place was crowded. Two girls boogied naked on the stage, kissing and playing with each other. The drunks loved it. I recognized the music: "Redemption Song" by Bob Marley. It was loud.

"Emancipate yourself from mental slavery.

None but ourselves can free our minds…
Some say it's just a part of it.
We must fulfill the book.
So won't you help to sing?
These songs of freedom
Cause all I ever have
Is redemption songs, redemption songs, redemption songs . . . ."

The disk got stuck and kept repeating and repeating. Fuck redemption. I'm going to kill that son-of-a-bitch—I'm going to kill him.

"redemption songs, redemption songs, redemption songs…"

Could I kill him? Or would he kill me? I banged into the jukebox and went psychopath on it: kicked it and shook it until the disc scratched and the tune died. Someone clubbed me over the head, put me in a headlock, and dragged me to the entrance. One bouncer held my arms; a second one punched me twice in the stomach. I went limp and sucked for air. They each grabbed a leg, an arm, and tossed me out the door like a common wino. I landed face down in the mud, head bleeding, the tip of the machete sticking into my thigh through the cheap canvas sheath. People laughed and pointed.

I struggled to my knees and vomited. Snot shot out my nostrils like a geyser. I mopped up the dangling slobber with the front of my shirt. Took a deep breath, and another. With my head bleeding and my vision blurred, I knelt in the street trying to focus. Two hookers tried to get me to stand. Each one reached under an arm and heaved up, then released me. I staggered, listed, and collapsed to my knees again. One girl ran back next to me. "Mira loco, sal de la calle que te va matar un carro." I laughed like a drunken idiot then abruptly stopped and growled at her.

The other girl jumped in. "O un caballo."

"A horse?" I laughed again, still kneeling in the street. Then the other girl said not to laugh, that a horse had broken loose during the parade. A little girl was in its path but someone had grabbed her in time.

The farthest slut jumped back in. "But no one is going to save you, borracho." I turned my head and stared her down. Anger sobered my gaze.

"Especially not a soldier," the puta next to me said.

I leaped into the air and onto my feet. "What soldier?"

"El Soldado, the hero who saved the little girl. He was dressed in fatigues. I know him."

"Where is he? You mean Larosa?"

"Larosa, si. All the girls know him."

"Where is he?" I reached in my pocket and pulled out some bills.

"Hay, Papi vamos . . . fucky-fucky?"

"No…where is he?" I held out a twenty.

She snatched it from my hand and tried to run but her heels sank in a muddy pothole. I grabbed her by the hair and pulled. We collided, and with my drunken momentum, I fell forward with the slut under me. She screamed like a rape victim. I flipped her on her back. "Where . . . is . . . he?" She kept yelling, swinging and slapping. The other slut jumped on my back and started scratching at my eyes. The three of us wrestled in the street like drunken idiots: the first girl on her back with me on top gripping both wrists and the other with both arms tugging at my neck—a slut sandwich. Finally, the one on my back caught an elbow in the jaw and ran off crying. I crammed my face up

217

against the one beneath me and squished my nose against her nose and slurred in a whisper. "Where is he?"

"You want to know? He is in the next cantina, cabron." She pointed and turned her face away, sobbing.

My heart started pounding. I tucked the twenty inside her cheek, evaded her attempt to bite my fingers, and marched to the porch.

This place was empty. Everyone on the block was at the bar I'd just been tossed out of. I rubbed the top of my head and wiped the blood from the clubbing off on my jeans. A raised knot two or three inches long graced the crown of my skull. What the hell had that bouncer hit me with? Through the front window of the vacant bar, I saw the bartender watching TV— soft-porn. I walked in.

"Que diablo tu quieres? No vez que estoy cerrado?" He was skinny and sweaty.

"Si, si perdona. Busco, El Soldado. Lo conoces?" I said

"Si, ya se fue al monte," he said, waving one hand and pointing at the door with the other.

"Soy su amigo. Donde en el monte?' I persisted. But he had turned back to his movie. The vaquero in the flick was raping a young girl. "Donde en el monte? Soy su amigo." I prodded on, knocking mud off my jeans on his floor.

He bitched at me again, then took a good look at my filthy clothes and the blood trickling from my head and lowered his voice. He said the chief stayed with his girlfriend near the barracks for the workers of the banana plantation on the slope, a house with the statue of the Virgin Mary in the front. He said I couldn't miss it; straight up the road to the highway and up the hill to the workers' tenement. The cantina-girls' huts were directly in front surrounded by the banana field.

Incredible . . . in the very plantation I'd waited at in the dark, though on the opposite end. I asked for tequila. He filled a shot glass. I gave him a ten dollar bill, fired it down, slammed the glass on the counter, and staggered to the end of the street wondering what time it was.

Somehow, after bickering with whores and passer-bys, I found the road back to the highway and marched to the end where the banana field started. The road went straight up the hill, just as the bartender had said. Bongos echoed up the mountainside from the illuminated square.

I slumped up the muddy road in front of lines and lines of banana stocks. Rows of giant, dark slender leaves flapped with the ocean breeze. With each step, I muttered Roby's name. Half a mile up, I found the section of little hut-houses and crouched in the road, studying the lay of the land.

The square plywood shacks had heavy corrugated aluminum lean-to roofs. The first two or three had little yellow porch lamps, swarming with moths. Farther up, a two-story tenement was lit up with a spot light from a tall pole. Hundreds of moths swarmed that light. I brushed away a fly . . . and another. There was no moon. The air was cool and brisk. A gaggle of hens and chirping little chicks scattered as I approached.

Ten shacks were lined up next to the road directly in front of the plantation. About two truck lengths separated one den of iniquity from the next. The first hut had several strange statues in front; the second a broken one. Outside the third a Jack Russell terrier growled and charged, yapping and yelping. A second and a third mutt shot out from the underneath the fourth hut and joined the first. The rat-terriers surrounded me, snapping and nipping at my heels. I thought of my parents and going to church with them to pray for Roby. I kept a steady stride. Two mutts stayed behind; the biggest followed me.

A girl sauntered from the fifth hut, topless. She waved and sipped on a beer. "Aqui muchacho, aqui." She slipped her hand in her panties. I kept moving. She laughed and threw the bottle in my direction, then went back inside. Could I really kill the chief? Could I do it? Are you a killer, cabron? The terrier stopped, gave one last yap and went back to his post.

At the sixth hut two naked kids on the porch were pawing at a kitten. A round woman waved. A little brown girl with stringy black hair came running toward me, shirtless and barefoot. She stopped beside the road to watch me pass. Without looking, I pulled a bill from my muddy pocket and held it out. The urchin-girl smiled, took it, and ran back to fat woman, who snatched it from her. A man lay passed out in front of the seventh shack. Two girls were going through his pockets. The last three huts were dark.

A white statue of Mary holding Jesus in her arms stood a few feet in front of the very last one. Flowers scattered the mud and melted candles surrounded her. This was the hut the bartender described. A little farther up was the long two-story barracks with the giant spotlight. Now I could also see bats; dozens of them, swooping down on the blinded moths. I gripped the handle of the machete, squeezed it, and pressed on. I gazed at the statue in the dark. Mary stared back at me.

As I stepped up onto the porch, I heard slapping and a girl moaning from inside. The door was unlocked. I pushed it open.

They were in the back room. She was whining loud as he spanked her. "Si, si, mas hay Papi, hay hay." The floor was a concrete slab. I could see the profile of a man on his knees fucking a girl doggy-style on a creaky mattress. He clutched both her arms with one hand and slapped her ass with the other as he pumped her. I inched up carefully, silently, closer.

The bedroom entrance had a curtain of red beads. Candles lit the little room, making the cheap beads into glowing rubies that flickered with the draft. I thought of Roby's photograph next to the candle at Mom's house. My breath quickened. My heart beat faster. Was it really him? It looked like him. Could I keep my promise? Lord help me. Help me kill. I tensed my jaw and bit down, then cautiously parted the beads with my left hand and slipped through.

It was him. Definitely him. His black ponytail was bouncing; this was his bronzed muscular back. The girl went limp and heaved out a long sigh; he kept pumping. With every plunge the mattress squeaked and she moaned again. He shoved her face into the pillow as he gripped her hair. A thrust; he paused. A thrust; another pause. Then he arched into her, holding her raised ass, and bowed his head and groaned and rested his forehead on her back.

The moment of silence swelled the hate inside of me. This was it, Lord forgive me. Now . . . do it now.

I yelled, "Soldado!" He jerked his head up off her arched back, rolling his heavy eyes like a drugged bull ready for the bullfighter's thrust.

My roaring swing whacked the blade into the nape of his neck with every ounce of crazed strength in my body. It severed his jugular; blood spurted over me and the sheets. He gasped and tumbled off the mattress. His arms flapped at his neck for a moment as blood poured out. His head dangled to one side. Blood rolled out like a stream of fertilizer from a grab-bucket. His cock shrivelled. He began convulsing. Blood soaked the concrete. He lay flat on his back; his neck twisted and his black ponytail faced me. I stabbed him in the gut several times. Each time, his body jerked.

Suddenly the girl came to her senses. She jumped off the bed and made a dash for the door. My left forearm nailed her mouth and her feet came out from under; she landed flat on her back, spitting blood. "No me mates—no me mates." She whimpered and stared at me with her junky-eyes. Blood dripped from my machete. The soldier was motionless. The candles fluttered.

"Sh sh sh." I dropped onto her chest and put the bloody blade on her neck and pressed the edge against her skin; one hand over her mouth. "Sh sh sh." I scanned the candlelit room, then looked down at her again.

Her eyes grew wide. She mumbled into my palm. "No me mates—no me mates."

Her body glistened in the candlelight. She was young. Her frantic, dizzy eyes excited me. I stuck three fingers inside her, pushed into her g-spot, clenched her pubic bone, and lifted her ass off the concrete floor while pressing the blade to her throat. She pissed. And I was the hand of God? Giggling came from the distant hut.

I wiped my wet hand on her face and hair, and whispered in her ear. "No viste nada. Solamente una sombra." She didn't move.

I scrambled to the front door and spied out the grounds— nobody. Everyone slept or fucked. Mouth wide open, gasping, I looked back at the girl and the contorted corpse. Jesus Christ. Get out of here. I checked the grounds again. It was still dark but daybreak was close. Couldn't go back through town. Go. Run. Run through the fields . . . up the mountain.

I darted from the porch and behind the tenement into the plantation. Bloody weapon in hand, I sprinted beneath giant banana stocks to a tractor road for harvesting the fields. I followed that uphill. Primordial grunts bellowed from inside me as I scuttled up and up.

At the crest, I stopped and retched, cried, retched again. My hand smelled; I tasted blood. I was covered in blood. Shit—had to get rid of the bloody clothes. Across a cleared track of land, a pile of brush big as a house was smoldering. A bulldozer was parked beside it. I dashed to the pile, shoved the blade of the machete into the dirt, and wiped it clean. Then stepped into the brush-pile and buried it, deep under heavy branches.

I stripped down to boots and underwear. The blood on my boots I daubed mud over, on my skin too. I gathered armfuls of dry grass, wrapped my stained clothes in it, and threw the bundle on top of the embers. I waited a few moments until it smoked, more and more; the breeze coming from behind me. The cloud of smoke grew, but I inhaled fresh air.

The wind shifted. The pile burst into flames and singed the hair on my legs. I gathered more grass and branches until the flames rose. I watched it burning and pictured the chief's neck dangling; blood oozing. Jesus Christ.

Satisfied with my fire, I bolted in boots and underwear down the slope. This side had not yet been cleared; the brush was thick. Branches snapped as I ran full stride down the back side of the mountain. I am the shadow. The shadow. I breathe the air of bears. I am a ghost on the wind. I am liquid. I am stone. I am fire. I am earth. I am light. I am night. I am right. I am truth. I am the shadow. I fell and scraped knees; banged my head. Branches whipped my face and slashed my skin. I felt nothing.

At the bottom, exhausted, I tried braking my strides but tumbled into a stream instead. I began wildly splashing water over my head and the back of my neck. I rinsed my boots and obsessively scrubbed all the blood I could or couldn't see. I cleansed every inch of skin, boots, and underwear, obsessed, like Lady Macbeth. After I was clean, I started swatting at flies and bugs, and kept swatting until I became aware of my nakedness.

I followed the stream downhill. All water eventually runs to the sea. Dawn's light appeared, and a house a mile downstream. In a vegetable garden fifty yards from a mud-brick hut, a scarecrow in a green army shirt guarded the crop. On a clothes line strung between trees, hung pants and t-shirts. I snagged the shirt from the scare-crow and a pair of shorts off the line, and snuck off.

I made my way to the autopista and started hitchhiking toward Maracaibo. Maybe I could find Tomas. I had no passport; it was on *Trader*. If I could get on a boat and sail to Mexico, I could swim the Rio Grande into the States. What else? The deed was done. I had kept my promise.

But now I was the killer.

23:
THE PRIEST
Veracruz, Mexico: Two Years Later

I never found Tomas in Maracaibo, but I made it to Mexico scrubbing decks aboard another shrimp boat and settled into Veracruz, working on the docks. I loaded containers for a year. On Saturday nights, in one of the warehouses, the dockworkers held bare-knuckled fights for money. That was how I got my first meal when I arrived, and I often went back.

By some twist of fate, I ran into Lupe one day, one of Coño's young twin brothers. He was moving bales of weed through the docks and had stayed to watch a bout. I cornered him, and to save his own ass, he divulged a terrible secret. Coño had been the one who'd actually killed my brother. Not that the chief was innocent. No. El Soldado had not been innocent. But Lupe's words stunned me, and I let him go. I spent another year looking for Coño but never found him. I grew homesick.

***

So today I have strolled up to the adobe-brick little church in a village square. It is a modest church with an arched doorway, creaky tongue-and-groove floors, and rough wooden benches.

"And so now you know my story, Padre. And I've been living here since. I'm obsessed with this deed. It haunts my sleep."

"To kill is a terrible sin. It is just that you suffer." The priest speaks through the wooden grate inside the holy booth. The booth is dark rosewood. The priest's breath smells like salsa. A rosary hangs around his white collar; a silver cross glitters in his hands as he speaks.

"I dread being awake. I dread my dreams. This is my affliction. This is why I'm here to see you. When I sleep, I mean if I sleep, because I only fall into sleep after days of insomnia, and then I fall out, and I wake up in a sweat. And, the first thing I'm conscious of is this guilt I carry in the back of my mind, and the back of my skull itches down to the nape of my neck all the time. It's always with me, in the color red, in dark rooms with candles, in screaming. If anyone screams near me I break into a nervous sweat and my breathing quickens—or, if a strange someone brushes too close in the street . . . Sometimes I dream I'm covered with flies and buried in a coffin, and I hear maggots chewing, and I wake brushing away the flies. . . . "

"Slow down, my son. Slow down." He rubs his thumb over the figure of Jesus on his cross.

"You see, Padre, I needed to speak to someone who knows about redemption. I need to speak to a virtuous man because I am obsessed with my own evil. It haunts my conscience and so I came to ask you—a priest—I came to ask this question I have— you are bound to me in oath—right, Padre?"

"Go ahead, my son. Ask." His aged, cracked voice whispers. How many confessions has he heard?

"Well—as I said, I was once a good man. I was raised by loving parents. I was in college—a student of philosophy. I know Kant's Universal Imperative: to treat the humanity in others, and Plato's doctrine of the Good and the Beautiful, and. . . ."

"Quiet your mind. Then ask your question."

"Yes, Padre. If a man has been good all his life, then commits sin—can this sin be washed? Can he be redeemed? I have committed all of the seven deadly sins and broken God's greatest commandment—for love of family—for justice."

"My son, you're in a confessional in God's house, and I function as His ears on earth."

"So you're bound by your oath not to report my sin—right, Padre?"

"Si. But I will not protect a criminal."

"I've told you my reason. I am no criminal." I glare into the grate and the voice behind it.

He leans back in his chair and the darkness in the booth obscures his face. His hand holds out the big silver cross. "Do you read the word of God?"

"Not lately, Padre."

"Well, pay attention. We are all God's children. But if you read Genesis carefully you will see it was Adam and Eve who were made in His image . . . not us. But they sinned and were cast out to fend for themselves. In Jeremiah, you can read that since we came from Adam and Eve, the human heart is basically evil."

"So I'm evil, Padre?"

"We are all sinners. Some more than others. And the universe is forever spinning out of control. We must accept the world as it is. Violence, even with just intentions, always rebounds on itself. See how you suffer."

"I do suffer, Padre."

"The Inquisition used to cleanse sinners through suffering. Their methods were unsound, but they understood that the human heart only learns by torment. There is little difference between men. But what difference there is—is very important. And the difference is acquired through suffering.

"Are you following me, my son? The Lord allows suffering to exist and thus we learn."

"Perhaps so, Padre, perhaps so."

"You come to me to be cured of this dread . . . this guilt . . . this affliction, as you call it. Yet it is this very suffering that has brought you to God's house. Is it not? If you were not suffering, you'd be out sinning instead of seeking. Do you see what I mean?"

"Yes Padre, I think so." I lean my sweaty forehead against the grating. Is there a fly buzzing in here with us?

"When a person suffers for acts he committed, he feels shame and guilt. The shame brings more suffering, and leads him to do what is necessary to remove it. Like coming here today. So suffering is the path to salvation—an awaking, a rebirth. Remember, we only comprehend darkness because we stood in the Sun's light."

"Yes, that's true, Padre."

"If life were easy, what would we learn from it? Nothing. So live with your affliction . . . with your dread. Accept the world as it is. Remembering your deed, and suffering from it, will make you do good things. They will accumulate and bring you peace."

"I will try, Padre. Gracias." I don't believe him but being in the church, hearing his serene, kind voice, and just having someone listen, makes me forget for a moment.

Then the priest tells me to turn myself in.

He never saw my face, but he heard my name. I storm out from the confessional and run into the street. He shouts after me, coming out of the confessional, but I do not turn back.

Instead I run to the bus station and sit panting on a bench across from a school. I watch teenage boys in blue uniforms playing baseball. There is a play at home plate and the catcher tags the runner out. I stand, clap, cheer. I think about Roby. Only the blue face remains on his watch. It hangs from a chain around my neck, laced through the remaining bracket. It doesn't tick anymore and has no arms or crystal, but I hold on to it. When I see my folks, I'm going to church with them . . . and pray for Roby.

Accept things as they are, the old priest said. Leave it to the Lord and wait, my mom had said.

The kids playing baseball change sides for the next inning, and my bus arrives. I keep thinking of Coño running loose and the chief dead, and Roby dead. Waiting for justice is hard. Goodness is in right action, and in having courage for those who are weak and can't help themselves. Again I remember Machiavelli's maxim, and the day Tomas and I were forced to swim for our lives.

A man who wishes to make a profession of goodness in everything must necessarily come to grief among so many who are not good. Therefore, it is necessary...to learn how not to be good and use this knowledge and not use it, according to the necessity of the case.

Today, I'll leave Veracruz and go Matamoros to swim El Rio, and return home.

THE END

Acknowledgements

For this book I owe thanks to my father, Captain Julio Cesar Alonso, for taking me to sea; to my mother and brother for their love and support; to Dr. Bill Brubaker and Janet Burroway, my writing professors, and Dr. Eugene F. Kaelin, my philosophy professor at Florida State University, where my writing began. To my writing professor Lenore Hart, and to my mentor, Captain David Poyer, at Wilkes University, where the book came to fruition. He freed me from the doldrums, plotted the course, and set me underway. And thanks to Dr. Bonnie Culver and Dr. J. Michael Lennon, and the many talented instructors for this great program and the access it provides.

About the Author

Julio Cesar Alonso Jr. was born in La Habana, Cuba, where his father commanded the Naval Air force Base in Mariel. The family fled from Castro when JC was three, landing in Miami, where he grew up. His father became a cargo ship captain, and so began JC's connection to the merchant marine. He spent summers at sea working as a deckhand and later a helmsman. JC has worked on bulk carriers, container ships, tankers, and RO/RO vessels, and was dock supervisor for Antillean Marine. JC received BAs from FSU in psychology and in creative writing. He taught at Miami Dade Community College for fourteen years, and earned a MS in counselling from Nova Southeastern. He received his MA and MFA degrees from Wilkes University. He now lives in South Florida where he fishes and dives with his brother. His poetry has been published in *Poetry Quarterly* and *Haiku Journal* and a short story received mention in *The Atlantic Monthly*. He presently teaches at Nova Southeastern University. This is his first novel.

Northampton House Press

Established in 2011, Northampton House Press publishes selected fiction, nonfiction, memoir, and poetry. Check out our list at www.northampton-house.com, and Like us on Facebook – "Northampton House Press" – as we showcase more innovative works from brilliant new talents.